Aviva
&
The Synagogue of Shanghai

CHIDELIA R. EDOCHIE

Copyright © 2016 Chidelia R. Edochie

All rights reserved.

ISBN-13: 978-0998119779
ISBN-10: 0998119776

CONTENTS

Part 1: From Paris, With Love
Paris, October 1941

Part 2: Mr. Chen's Restaurant & Café
Shanghai, November 1941

Part 3: Aviva & The Synagogue of Shanghai
Shanghai, December 1941

Part 4: Goodbye to the Dark

Part 1: From Paris, With Love

October 1941, Paris

1

From Aviva Druker's window in Paris in 1941, she watched as a man plummeted to his death, his neck attached to a noose, his feet greeting the air, while a French policeman and a German SS officer stood together atop the gallows in casual conversation, smoking a ciggie.

She had been sitting with her daughter, Ora, in her lap and writing in her journal—*Am I too young for this marriage, too young for this child, too young for this war? Is time with me, or is it against me?* She heard gunshots go off in the distance, and had come to the window to close it. Their apartment was on the first floor of the building and their front door opened out directly onto the street, rue de Pasteur, and the living room windows provided a clear view of her neighborhood and of the square less than a block away. The square had once been a friendly meeting ground of old people lounging on wrought iron benches and mothers lazily watching their children toddle by, but now was a meeting ground for the everyday business of a Nazi-occupied city: list making, name taking. Neck breaking.

Now, Aviva found herself watching the SS officer as he hopped down from the gallow stage — *hopped* down, like a boy from a fence — and rapped his knuckles against the toe of the hanged man's boot to make sure he was really dead.

Aviva shut the window and closed the drapes, then buried her face in their thick fabric, her body shaking. She'd always been called a waif, told that her big eyes and petite body and reddish-brown hair made her look like a small deer. But what people really meant when they described her that way was that she looked weak. She was weak, and she knew it. And in this war, she was reminded of her weakness every single day. But it wasn't only her. Everyone in Paris, everyone in France, everyone in Europe was aware of their weaknesses now.

She looked down at her daughter, Ora, perched on the floor. Barely two years old, still mostly gurgling rather than speaking, innocent and oblivious. Aviva was twenty-two. She thought that having a child, being a mother, would turn her into a fully grown woman. To protect someone so small should make her feel bigger. But she didn't. *Am I too young for this war?*

Aviva picked the child up and held her tightly to her chest, her eyes darting around the tiny, dark apartment. Her husband, Samuel Druker, had already sold off most of their furniture in preparation for their departure from France, a departure that he still, in fact, had not yet planned. He was a vague, anxious man, the kind of man who sold off the furniture before figuring out where they were going to live next. In the center of the room sat their luggage, already packed. The suitcases were mostly all cracked and dull, except for the antique valise that had belonged to her mother. It was a small trunk painted a rich, deep red with cream-colored flowers vining up its sides. It was the only thing her mother had left her when she died.

Suddenly, three sharp knocks reverberated against her front door. For a moment she thought it was gunfire. The knocks came again, and this time Aviva quickly put Ora into her crib and sprang into action. There was a series of steps that she and Samuel had worked out since the Nazi's had taken Paris: she peeked through a sliver of curtain to see if a car had pulled up outside (one hadn't); she checked to see if the table cloth adequately covered the hidden compartment (it did); she took out their birth certificates, which had already been packed away, and confirmed that they were the ones with their parents' altered names, un-Jewish (they were).

She started toward the door. Then, she saw it: her husband's kippah. The soft, brimless cap that Samuel wore when he prayed was sitting on the coffee table in the front room; he must have left it out after that morning's prayer. She grabbed the kippah from the table, quickly rolled it up, and stuffed it into the front pocket of her dress as the persistent knocks at the door turned into loud, hard whaps. *Is time with me, or is it against me?*

She looked through the spyhole and drew a breath: it was a man, tall and strong, in a German officer's uniform, his back to the door. The red, black, and white Nazi armband was wrapped tightly around a bicep, screaming his affiliation. She watched as his head turned in quick hard angles as he looked up and down the street, waiting for her to open the door, confident of her silent presence inside.

Aviva opened the door only a crack, and the German officer immediately whipped toward her with a sharpness that made her step back. His broad face seemed carved from stone, and he gripped a portfolio stuffed with papers in one large, white hand.

"Confirming the Vichy census," he said, his voice

like the loud bark of a dog on a hunt. "Are you Mrs. Druker?" he asked her. "Are you here alone?"

Instead of answering him, she glanced anxiously up and down the street. Pedestrians kept their heads down as they passed by her door, and some even crossed to the other side, moving away from her and the German as subtly and as quickly as they could. A neighbor across the road and down a few buildings — Laurienne, her best friend of two years — dropped the broom she'd been using to sweep her steps, scurried into the safe darkness of her home, and slammed the door behind her with a loud, deserting thud.

Aviva looked into the face of the German officer, and he stared back at her intently with cold, sea-foam eyes.

"Yes," she said. "I'm alone."

"May I enter?" he asked, and without waiting for an answer he pushed past Aviva and entered her living room.

Her stomach met with her heart in her chest, and after a final quick glance out at the rapidly emptying streets and quiet apartments where eyes were probably peering at her from behind closed curtains, she shut the door, and allowed herself to be trapped inside with him.

In the middle of a small, shabby apartment in Paris, France, Officer Erik von Strommer—German, male, somewhat Lutheran, thirty years—stood over the crib of Ora Druker—French, female, Jewish, eighteen months—who looked up at him with a strange sort of self-possession. Fearless. Not yet aware of the concept of fear.

Erik had only made it to Paris because of his father's influence: Oscar von Strommer, founder of the largest printer and publishing house in Berlin. Not a soldier himself during the Great War—he'd feigned a more serious form of asthma than what he truly suffered—the senior von Strommer earned the gratitude of the National Socialist German Worker's Party by offering his new printing technology to mass produce their pamphlets. Thus, when it was time for Erik to join their ranks, the junior von Strommer's request to be sent to the city of art and romance instead of to the eastern front was quickly granted.

The little girl's mother, Aviva Druker—also French and Jewish, twenty-two years old but she seemed like a girl to him—crept slowly up behind him as he gazed down at her child.

"She's so small," Erik said without turning around, and Aviva thought to herself, *I know this man's back better than I know his front.*

"Yes," she agreed. Whatever he said, she would agree.

She reached to pick up her daughter, but before she could, Erik turned and took Aviva into his arms, and pressed his mouth forcefully onto hers.

She resisted, but only for a moment, then melted into him. They didn't break away until a soft wail rose from Ora's crib beneath them.

"You shouldn't be here," Aviva said weakly as she finally broke away from him and picked up the crying child. "My neighbors…," she said.

But Erik wasn't listening.

"I've got it all figured out, Aviva," he said as he paced excitedly. The stoniness was gone now, dropping away from like a coat, and now his face grew flush and buoyant. The dingy room too small for his broad body. His eyes only landed on any one thing for a split-second at a time.

"We'll leave Paris tomorrow night," Erik was saying, "and make our way to the Swiss border. I've already paid the checkpoint guards."

He was Odysseus leaving Troy; he was Jason assembling his Argonauts..

"Then from there," he continued, "we can go

wherever we want. To America or —"

"And Ora, too, right? She's allowed?" Aviva asked, anxiety like pebbles in her throat. "You told them we'll have a child with us?"

Erik looked away from her, then crossed over to the window to peak out. He replied without turning back around.

"Of course I have."

He eyed the small mound of luggage at the center of the room.

"Though *this*," he said, sweeping a hand toward the suitcases, "might be too much to carry with us."

Aviva told him that Samuel had been packing them all up. "He says we must leave as soon as possible," she said. "Now that Jews are being arrested."

She stole a glance at her German lover, then corrected herself. "Now that *we're* being arrested."

Erik didn't reply to her light accusation, and they fell into an awkward silence. He seemed to hate it when she brought up the differences between them, but how could she not? Every day more news filtered in from Germany, from Poland, from Russia. Whatever the fate was of the Jewish people in those countries could be her fate, too. Could be Ora's. She'd told herself that that was why she had allowed this German man to fall in love with her. And did she love him, too? She didn't know. But he's seemed to be a man of action, a man who made plans and then made them happen, and he was what she needed if she wanted to get out of France, to save Ora's and her own life. Samuel couldn't do it. He'd been talking about since the day the Germans had officially occupied Paris, and had continued talking about it since the Nazi's had started making lists of Jewish families. But he hadn't *done* anything.

Erik took Ora from her mother and cuddled the child for a brief moment, before returning her to the crib. Then he drew Aviva to him, determined to keep the mood light.

"In Switzerland it won't matter that you are Jewish, or that I am German," he said. "Or that you are such a horrible dancer."

Finally Aviva laughed, glad for some distraction, however brief. The worry that had been etched into her face slightly softened.

"I told you," she said, "I never learned."

"I'll teach you now."

He wrapped an arm around her tiny waist and

gave it a gentle squeeze, rocking her body from side to side. Aviva leaned into him, almost ready to give in to his escapism. But a sense of dread still clung to her. She couldn't shake it.

"There were hangings today," she said. "I could see them from my window."

Erik broke away from her with a frustrated sigh. He felt like she was blaming him. Didn't she know by now that he wasn't like the others? He started pacing again.

"*Yes*, the police are starting to round up local Jews," he said, as talking about some petty annoyance like the rising cost of petrol. "And *yes*," he continued, "Resistance fighters are being hanged." He stopped pacing and turned on her. "But that's why we're leaving, Aviva!"

He crossed back over to where Aviva stood, and as he approached he noticed that she took a step backward, away from him. He softened his voice.

"That's why I'm taking you and Ora out of here," he said. "You just have to trust me."

From the crib, Ora began to wail again and Aviva moved to pick her up, trying and failing to bite back tears. As she passed by him, Erik took her arm and pulled her against his chest.

"I'm sorry, my love," he said. "I'm just tired. Tired of this war."

She stayed silent, refusing to look at him.

"I got in trouble with my lieutenant yesterday," Erik said, trying desperately to change the direction of things. "He caught me writing a sonnet for you while I was on duty."

She finally looked up at him, and studied his face. It was the face of a man who might genuinely love her.

"A sonnet?" she said, sounding like a child even to her own ears. "For me?"

She leaned into him again, this time letting herself dissolve with him completely.

"I *do* trust you," she whispered.

A burst of machine gunfire went off in the distance, nearer than before. She buried her face into his chest, trying to block out the sound of bullets firing, trying not to imagine where the bullets were landing. But they were so loud.

"It's getting closer and closer," she whispered.

Erik kissed her on the forehead, almost paternally, and spoke to her with the confident tone that he knew she needed from him.

"It will never touch us."

2

Later that afternoon, after Erik was gone, Aviva sat on her steps idly watching as a young boy expertly emptied trash bins, methodically reaching into each can to remove any trapped garbage, unafraid of the possibility of his hands grazing some mysterious sludge. She tried to read the face of everyone who passed by to see if they regarded her with suspicion over Erik's brief visit. But no one even glanced at her. A local police car rolled by, what Parisians had nicknamed *Gretels* since they were now driven by German-commanded hands, and it was followed closely by a *Hansel*, what they called the German military trucks. White faces peered out of the Hansel and out of the Gretel, but the cars did not stop. Ora slept soundly against her shoulder, and Aviva breathed in the smell of her milky breath as the garbage boy moved on to the next can at the end of the street, slinging his bag over one shoulder like an American 1920's hobo she'd seen on the cover of an old pulp novel.

Across the street and down a few buildings, her neighbor Laurienne emerged from her own apartment building, spotted Aviva, and rushed over to her.

When Aviva had moved into Samuel's home after their wedding, Laurienne had been the first person to knock on her door and introduce herself. Laurienne's toddler son had clutched at his mother's skirt and looked wide-eyed at Aviva as Laurienne implored her to come out and have a smoke on the steps and gossip. Aviva didn't smoke, but Laurienne didn't hold that against her. From the beginning Aviva had tried to follow Samuel's decree that they keep to themselves, lest any of their neighbors realize their Jewishness. But Aviva was lonely, and she had always felt confident that Laurienne wouldn't care if she knew. Although, since France had fallen to the Germans, Laurienne had become a little more withdrawn, more secretive. But so had everyone. Now, she was standing over Aviva with her arms crossed against her chest, and Aviva held her breath.

"What did that German want at your door this morning?" Laurienne asked in a low voice, keeping her eyes on the pedestrians ambling by. "Was he asking about Gus?"

A surge of relief briefly paralyzed Aviva's mind. When a fellow Parisian saw you talking to a German, they didn't worry about you. They worried about what you could be saying about *them*.

"About your husband? No, no," said Aviva reassuringly. She tried to keep her voice steady. She was still new to lying. "Just confirming our census information. You know, 'how long have you lived here?' That sort of thing."

She patted the space next to her on the steps and Laurienne sat down, her face plainly awash with the relief and guilt that Aviva hoped was not visible in her own eyes.

"Good," Laurienne said, her relief plain. "*Merci a Dieu.*" She made a cross sign over her chest with one hand and removed a lighter and a pack of *Gauloises* with the other.

"I never told you," Laurienne said slowly, "because I didn't want to cause you and Sam any trouble."

Then Laurienne fell silent, and Aviva watched as puffs of smoke from her mouth evaporated into the air. She realized that her friend — her *only* friend — was waiting for her to pry, to demand to know the secret, so that she, Aviva, could share the burden of it. And perhaps to take some responsibility for whatever consequences the revelation might cause.

"Never told me what?" asked Aviva.

The stones that made up their street, rue de Pasteur, sometimes absorbed sound, sometimes bounced it around. Its residents seemed to know exactly which positions, which gusts of wind, and what amount of foot traffic was best for telling secrets one wanted kept, and which positions were best for secrets that one did not want kept.

Laurienne glanced around, leaned close to Aviva but turned her face away from her, and waited a moment for a soft breeze to come wafting down the road. A secret she wanted kept.

"It's Gus," said Laurienne. "He's been writing pamphlets. Against the Germans. He passes them out to people I don't trust."

When Laurienne turned her face back to Aviva's, she was looking into the wet, fearful eyes of her strong, rather bossy friend.

"I know one day he'll get us all carted off to jail," Laurienne went on, "or worse."

Aviva was about to respond, to reassure her, but the door to Laurienne's apartment building suddenly opened, and out stepped Gus with their five-year-old son in tow. Gus was tall and handsome and walked with a proud gait, and Laurienne perked up at the sight of her husband, as if by habit. He and the little boy waved at the female pair before turning down the street toward the square, away from them. The women waved back and watched them go.

"He's passionate," Aviva said. "It must feel good to have plans, to fight for something." She was overly enthusiastic now, desperate to alleviate her friend's terribly valid fears. "Even if it's underground. Even if no one knows. It's good to fight."

Laurienne stubbed her cigarette out on the concrete step.

"Sometimes I dream of leaving him," she said. "Leaving our boy, too. Just running away."

Aviva felt Ora stirring in arms, and she watched as Gus lifted his son onto his shoulders without breaking his stride.

"Would you ever?" she asked Laurienne, watching as the father and son disappeared around a corner. "Run away from them?"

Laurienne followed Aviva's gaze, but her husband and son were already gone. The main door to Aviva's building opened from behind them, and a geriatric couple stepped out and toddled cautiously down the steps and onto the road without acknowledging the two young mothers. Laurienne watched them go, and Aviva was struck by the sudden intensity in her voice when she finally answered.

"Never."

3

That evening, Aviva rushed to make dinner before Samuel got home. She was a horrible cook, even before the occupation, when they still had butter. Every night it was like a game: she would wholeheartedly guess at which ingredients went well together, throw them in a pan, and hope for the best. If she had some treat from Erik—fresh coffee, a raspberry cake—she would have to find a way to explain its presence to Samuel, or else hoard it for herself to eat while he was at the bookshop. She wondered what Erik would say she was worse at: dancing, or cooking? She'd never cooked for him

She hummed as she worked, and realized that it was the tune she'd heard from Erik earlier that day. She went to Ora's crib, leaned over and hummed the nameless song down at her daughter until Ora smiled and gurgled up a laugh, causing a joy in Aviva that was so simple and clear that any doubt she'd had about getting her daughter out of Paris, out of France, out of Europe, disappeared. Before things got any worse.

There was only one choice: go. Leave. Britain wasn't safe, but there was America, there was Australia. Erik had the connections, not Samuel. Erik had the money, and so much of it. The day he'd asked her to leave with him, he'd shown her a briefcase filled with Swiss francs. She thought of the small, practically empty safe at the back of Samuel's fledgling bookshop. She had to get herself and her daughter out of Europe, and there was only one choice: go.

At seven o'clock sharp, Samuel scuttled through the door. He was already thirty-five when they married, shorter than her, with a round, olive-skinned face that always seemed crumpled up in anxious thought, framed by small, square eyeglasses. He was kind, mostly, but weak. She'd had the same thought every single day of their two years of marriage: he was kind, he was weak. Samuel dumped an armful of books onto the table, and wiped his shiny forehead with his sleeve as Ora babbled gleefully at her father's arrival, and Aviva realized that the baby was babbling the tune that she'd been humming to her.

"Oh, listen!" Aviva cried, reveling in her discovery. "Listen to Ora, she's almost singing—"

But Samuel cut her off, his expression dour.

"I've found our way out," he said.

Samuel usually spoke in such a way that Aviva was never sure whether he was making statement or asking a question. But now his voice was strong and sure, though he continued to move around in his normal, anxious way. He went to the window and drew the curtain closed, then removed his glasses and used one curtain to wipe the sweat from his brow, breathing heavily, as if he'd run home. Aviva had never seen him like this.

"Calm down," she said, slightly annoyed. "What is it?"

She was used to him coming home with stories of disappearances, arrests, attacks, the terrors to come, the terror already here. And then doing nothing about it. Ghost stories meant to make her afraid of things he couldn't protect them from her, her and Ora.

"*It's* Shanghai," he whispered.

As her mouth gaped open, he began to bustle about the room, opening and closing their luggage, taking things out, putting them back in. She followed him around, their living room so small that she could only move in tiny steps to avoid bumping into him from behind.

"'*It's* Shanghai,'" she repeated. "*What's* Shanghai?" She felt alarmed, she feltconfused. He wasn't making any sense.

But Samuel didn't stop.

"We've got to finish packing. The boat leaves in three days," he said. He was getting breathless again. Was he asthmatic? She'd never asked him before. "But we won't be allowed much luggage, Aviva," he went on. "We have to send our things ahead tomorrow. So we must pack!"

Aviva grabbed her husband's arm, halting his flurry of movement. She tried to look into his eyes, but could only see herself reflected back in his spectacles.

"Look at me, Sam," she said slowly, hoping that his brain would to its hurrying to match the pace of her words. "I can't understand you. *What* boat?"

With a strange look on his face — was it pride? — Samuel removed several small pieces of paper from his breast pocket. Tickets, but for what?

"It's a boat that will take us to Japan, then on to Shanghai," he said, speaking quickly. "No other countries are giving visas out to Jews, do you understand? But for Shanghai, we don't *need* visas. No one does. But only in Shanghai, understand? But to get there, we must first catch the train to the port in Marseille. It leaves the day after tomorrow. *Then* the boat. That's why we must *pack* Aviva. Pack!"

Aviva stood paralyzed in the center of the room while Samuel moved around her. Things were happening too fast. Erik's plan, Samuel's plan. Suddenly, everyone had a plan.

How long had he been thinking of this? Why hadn't he told her before? And why Shanghai? She knew why; he'd just told her. But still, she wondered, why?

Her mind raced. Switzerland sounded better to her. Plenty of money. Border guards already paid. Then on to America, or to wherever. It was too late to say no to Erik. It was too late to say yes to Samuel. Too late for Samuel to turn into the husband she'd needed before.

She sat down at the table and put her face into her hands. Ora was awake in her crib, but quiet.

"No," Aviva said quietly. "No. I won't go."

Samuel looked at his wife, not quite comprehending. They were going to Shanghai. That's where they were going. Death was coming for them in Paris, and there was only one choice: go.

"I won't get on a ship and go across the world," Aviva continued, almost wailing, "where I know *nothing*, where I know *no one*—"

Realizing now that his wife must have briefly lost her mind, Samuel sharply turned away from her and continued gathering up their things. He spoke to her over his shoulder, as if he couldn't bother to face her while she was in hysterics.

"We must," he said, sternly and simply. "You don't see the danger closing in around us. You're blind to it." He fanned through the pages of a book, looking for any loose letters, any documents that might look suspicious if found, before packing it away. "It's only a matter of time before someone, the police or a neighbor, guesses at what we really are."

She wrapped her arms around herself, trying to ignore the guilt and self-condemnation that tinged those last words: *what we really are.*

What was she, really? She was a woman—young, but still a woman, a mother—married to a man who up until this very moment had acted rather convincingly as if he couldn't save them. And now, suddenly, he could.

"No," she said again. "I won't go."

She rocked back and forth in her chair and pressed

her lips together, as if to prevent secrets from spilling out. Tomorrow night when it was time to abscond with Erik, she had imagined walking out the door with Ora while Samuel was still at work. And if he came home early, she would claim that Ora hadn't been out all day and needed a walk, for the fresh air. It wasn't much of a plan, she knew. The city air smelled of spilled blood and cannon smoke. There was nothing fresh about it. But that was her plan.

Samuel watched from across the room as Aviva rocked herself back and forth, back and forth. She was consoling herself, he realized, because he could not do it. Even though he was her husband, even though it was his duty. He'd never learned how to console a woman, and Aviva was more of a girl than a woman anyway. When Aviva's cousin, Ruby, had brought her to him to be his wife, he was already rather used to widowhood, accustomed to his quiet life of selling books and reading the daily newspaper, exchanging thoughts with himself. When he met Aviva for the first time, he'd had the feeling that he was adopting a child rather than getting married. Hadn't Aristotle said that the most appropriate age for marriage was around eighteen for girls, and thirty-seven for men? So, he and Aviva were testing the ancient philosophers. Proving them wrong.

He took a step toward her, then hesitated, reconsidered. Nothing separated them but the empty space of that dreary living room and a small pile of half-packed luggage, but to Samuel it felt like an impossible ravine. He removed the train and boat tickets from his pocket and laid them, one by one, on the battered coffee table.

"Do you know what I had to do to get these?" he asked Aviva quietly.

She didn't answer, but stopped rocking in her chair and looked at him.

"I sold my grandfather's *tallit*," he said.

Aviva gasped. In her mind flashed the ancient silk garment, beautifully woven in white and blue with gold-knotted fringe, the swathe of fabric hundreds of years old. It was sacred to him.

She went over to Samuel and stood over her husband, but still did not touch him.

"Sold?" she asked incredulously. "To who?"

"Some young man, he called himself an antiques dealer," he said. "I told him it was an antique rug, he didn't know the difference." Samuel breathed a heavy, grieving sigh. "Me, my father, my grandfather, and those before him. We all prayed with that *tallit* over our heads. Now that boy will probably throw it on the floor and wipe his feet with it."

Aviva kneeled down beside him and gazed at him piteously. She did not want to make him feel any worse, but she couldn't help but wonder the worst. What if the dealer *did* know what the tallit was? What if this young man—a stranger to them—knew that it wasn't a rug at all, knew perfectly well that its owner must be a Jew?

But she didn't voice these concerns, and instead placed a hand on her husband's back, and stroked it consolingly, the job of a wife.

Samuel looked up, surprised at her touch. Surprised by her closeness.

"It doesn't matter anymore," he said, the still newfound certainty returning to his voice. He stood up, pulling her up with him, and pointed at the tickets laid out on the table. "It was worth it," he said. "I would've sold myself to keep us out of harm's way."

He looked deeply at Aviva, and in his eyes she saw a strength he must have been hiding from her for two years.

Aviva didn't know what to say, or what to do. Her mind wanted to flee, to drift to Erik and his confident promises for her and little Ora's future. But here was Samuel, right in front of her, present in a way that he had never been before.

Suddenly they were interrupted by loud shouting outside. Aviva was glad for a reason to break away — she needed to think, she needed to breath — and rushed to the window to see what the commotion was all about. Like a child, she forgot to be afraid of what she might find.

Outside on the rue de Pasteur, a bloodied Gus was being dragged out of his building toward a truck by two policemen. He was fighting them the entire way. Samuel came up behind Aviva, and together they watched from their window as the scene unfolded.

Laurienne rushed outside behind her husband, her son in her arms and her face contorted in rage and worry. A third policeman immediately marched over to Laurienne and ripped her son out of her arms. Gus, seeing this, kicked one of the officers, and the policemen that'd been dragging him toward the truck immediately stopped to hurl down a tornado of punches to Gus's face, kicks to his stomach, batons to his groin. The third officer roughly placed Laurienne and Gus's son into the back of the truck.

As Aviva watched from her window, she had no particular idea in mind as to what would, or should, happen next. So, when Laurienne suddenly turned on her heel — *away* from her little boy, *away* from her beaten husband — and began to run down the street, Aviva neither understood nor rejected her friend's actions. Laurienne was running up the street, in the direction of Aviva and Samuel's building, and Aviva could see the wild look on the woman's face, the look of a hunted animal making an escape.

Laurienne, the one who sang opera while doing laundry in the alley, had only taken four or five strides when a single gunshot exploded from behind her. Aviva watched as blood spread across the front of her friend's dress — a dress she'd borrowed once — and then Laurienne toppled forward to the ground. Back at the truck, the third policeman stood with his pistol still raised, a soft curl of smoke drifting up from the muzzle.

Aviva's horrified eyes were riveted on Laurienne. Her body began to shake, but she didn't notice it until Samuel grabbed her by both arms to still her. She kept shaking, and continued to look at Laurienne's unmoving body until Samuel finally pulled her away from the window and shut the curtains once more.

Samuel wrapped his wife tightly into his arms, trying to still her, but it didn't work. He tried to soothe her by making long, low shushing sounds into her ear. It was rhythmic white noise, and after a few moments Aviva was actually listening to it, anticipating the next beat. Her body forgot itself, and she slowly went still in his arms.

Once she'd finally calmed, Samuel pulled her chin

up so that he was looking into Aviva's eyes.

"I'll never let that happen to us," he said.

Aviva felt something well up in her that was unrecognizable in its strength. Respect? Trust.

"I know," she said, gazing up at him. "I trust you."

Then Samuel—unromantic, unsentimental Samuel—broke away from her and started toward the kitchen.

"Come, let's do a prayer of protection for our journey," he said. "We need it now more than ever."

At the kitchen table, Samuel lifted a corner of the tablecloth and slid open the compartment where they hid the things that required hiding. But he found it empty.

Aviva had trailed behind him into the kitchen in a daze, still looking backward toward the closed curtain, still imagining Gus being beaten, Laurienne running toward her, their son in the back of the truck with his arms stretched out toward his mother.

When she looked back at her husband, she found him staring at her with a questioning gaze, holding open the hidden compartment of the table. It took her a moment to realize what he was looking for, and when she did, her face reddened. She couldn't meet her husband's eyes.

His *kippah*. She'd forgotten about it, how she'd grabbed it and stuffed it into her pocket earlier that day when Erik had knocked at the door.

She quickly shoved a hand into her dress pocket, removed the kippah and focused on unrolling and reshaping it as Samuel stared at her.

"Why was it in your pocket?" he asked. Not accusatory, not suspicious, an innocent question. But still she responded with a nervousness that made no sense, not to him.

"You left it out this morning," she said, stammering. She handed him the kippah, and he took it from her wordlessly.

A sudden surge of anger coursed through her, anger at his quiet nature, anger at his sudden ability to make plans, forcing her to reconsider her own.

"How could you have left it in plain sight like that way?" she cried. "Anyone could have seen it. You know how dangerous it is."

The shock from seeing her friend murdered just moments ago, the guilty evidence hiding in her dress pocket, all of it seemed to be exploding from her now, onto her husband.

"I'm sorry," he said.

An apology, his usual way of mollifying her. And just as suddenly as it had risen, the anger surged backward, from herself onto herself. She was ashamed, and she had so little time to process one feeling of shame before another emerged.

"It doesn't matter," she said, suddenly exhausted. "It doesn't matter anymore."

Aviva picked Ora up out of her crib. The child's eyes were wide open, as if she had been listening to her parents' argument and her mother's guilt and to the bullet that killed Laurienne with a benign sensitivity and acceptance.

Samuel stood with his wife and daughter and recited a prayer of protection. Outside, rue de Pasteur was quiet and totally empty except for Laurienne's unmoving body that had been left behind, still lying facedown, the back of her dress caked with drying blood.

Inside their home, Aviva watched her husband with quiet respect as he prayed, their hands clasped together as if they were exchanging wedding vows again.

Outside, a covered military truck rolled down their street. It stopped at Laurienne.

A thin, mustached policeman descended from the truck. He stared at Laurienne for a moment, then dragged her toward his truck and lifted her onto the covered bed. If Aviva were still watching from the window, she would see Laurienne being shoved through the slit of the truck's flapping doors and being added to a pile of dead bodies, all of their bare limbs entwined like white twigs in a bird's nest.

4

Later that night, Aviva lay in bed with her eyes wide open while Sam slept beside her, snoring deeply, peacefully. Aviva stared at the ceiling. She wished that the boat to Shanghai were leaving tomorrow, and that she and Samuel and their daughter were already safely on their way. *Shanghai*. Or she wished that Erik would tap on the window at that very moment, and that she and Ora could walk off with him into the darkness. She wished that there were stars for her to count. She wished that whatever was going to happen, that it would happen right now.

Finally, she got out of bed. She reached into the nightstand drawer, removed her journal, and crept into the living room.

She curled herself into a chair and opened her

journal, and a small piece of paper fell out and fluttered down to the floor. She rummaged around the dark room for a candle, lit it, and found the little gray square that had fallen.

It was a photo: Samuel in a suit, her holding Ora, both of them staring straight ahead, not grim, but not unhappy. A married couple, new parents. Black and white and gray.

Aviva looked at her small, dainty handwriting, and read the first line on the open page where the photo had been stuck.

When I saw him, we were standing in a line. I have been living my life in lines –

She slammed the journal shut. It was the day she met Erik; this was what she'd written on the day she met Erik.

She stood up and glanced around the dark, empty room. She could leave right now, all by herself, without Ora, without any of them. But there was a curfew.

So she sat back down. She opened the journal again. She decided to try and see herself as he, Erik, would've seen her. Perhaps the way Samuel saw her, too. What must they both think of her? She found the page again and read it, letting herself remember the day that a German soldier had broken into her life.

~

When she saw him, they were standing in a line. She had been living her life in lines since the occupation: a line for answering census questions (they lied), a line to hand over personal guns (they had none, but had to stand in the line anyway). In that first year after the occupation, it was these lines that bonded every Parisian to every other. They all had the same pain in their legs, the same stiffness in their backs, the same paper cuts on their fingers from sifting through document after document to prove that they were who they claimed to be, even when they weren't.

The line that day was a line to receive rather than to give: a food ration line. It was manned by French police officers but overseen by German soldiers. Everyone around her looked desperate and hungry, and she realized that she must look that way too. Samuel stood close behind her watching the German men anxiously. But she was calm; she knew how to draw into herself, to will her mind elsewhere. While hundreds of her fellow citizens jostled forward in the line toward a promise of stale bread and milk that was just beginning to spoil, she stepped forward mechanically, her expression remote, her eyes as empty as she could make them.

Erik saw her before she saw him. He'd been striding through the lines, scanning the faces impersonally, trying to look commanding while running stanzas of poetry through his head. Then, his eyes landed on one pale girl, hair the color of red-tinted honey, eyes like brown walnuts set wide in a heart-shaped face. She looked alien amongst the others. An older man hovered behind her. She held a baby in her arms with the casual authority of a mother, but that must be a mistake. She must have been minding the child for someone else; she was only a girl herself.

Erik moved to the head of their table just as Aviva and Samuel were up next. He wordlessly took the questionnaire from the French officer, who did not protest, who was tired from a long day of questioning his fellow citizens in exchanged for food the Germans themselves did not want. When Aviva and Samuel arrived to the head of the line, Erik stared intently at the top of Aviva's head while she looked down at the child in her arms, and then down at her own feet.

"Your name, miss?" Erik said kindly.

Samuel stepped forward and spoke. "We are—

But Erik cut him off. "I was speaking to the lady," he said, still staring at Aviva, speaking with such soft kindness that Aviva was startled out of her detachment. She looked up, and found herself staring into a handsome, broad face, a strong jaw, with sweet, watery eyes that pierced her own.

"I'm Aviva, sir," she said quietly, stammering a bit. But the intensity of his gaze seemed to enter her, filling her with something, and her voice quickly strengthened, and spoke again, louder this time. "I'm Aviva Druker."

Erik smiled down on her, as if they were all alone, as if there weren't a hundred people behind her in line and a hundred people waiting at the next table, and the next. The French officer drifted away from them like loose paper in the wind.

"And this is your little sister?" Erik asked, nodding to Ora. He glanced at Samuel. "And your father?"

Aviva could feel Samuel shifting behind her uncomfortably, weak waves of irritation and fear emanating off his body onto hers. She steeled herself against her husband's fretful, useless energy.

"No, sir," she said. "This my daughter, and this is my husband."

Samuel finally broke in into what felt like a private dialogue from which he was being blatantly excluded.

"My name is Samuel Druker," he said, so loudly that others in the next line looked at him strangely.

Bur Erik ignored him. He feigned a slightly chastising tone as he continued to smile down at the girl in front of him.

"But Miss Aviva," he teased, "you look far too young to be a wife and mother. You should be at the Sorbonne with the other students, penning leaflets and throwing rocks at bad Germans like me." With that he put a hand over his heart, as if his own Germnanness truly pained him, as if he would gladly take a rock to the head, as long as it came from her hand.

She couldn't help it, she laughed. It rang high and clear and the French officers at the tables nearby stared at her in disapproval. But when Erik stared back at them they looked away, returning to their own clipboards and long lines of hungry mouths.

Aviva thought of other German soldiers she'd seen patrolling her street, and the teenaged French girls they flirted with. If a local girl responded to German catcalls with so much as a smile, she'd heard the older neighbors and even Laurienne call them whores. Aviva, who had gone from her cousin's house to her husband's, had never been called a whore before. She had never learned to flirt. She'd never been romanced.

Behind her, Samuel fumbled with a folder of papers, pulled out a document, and thrust it at Erik.

"Our marriage license," he said, his voice now quiet and a little cold.

Erik took the document and reluctantly pulled his eyes from Aviva, who now looked at him with an open curiosity that bordered on longing as Erik skimmed the license.

"This is a copy from the courts," said Erik curtly, suddenly remembering himself and his duties. "French copies often lack the information we require." He looked sharply at Samuel. "Your religion?"

"Catholic," Samuel practically barked. He immediately realized his mistake, and so did Aviva, and so did Erik. He had again answered too loudly, too quickly. Too desperately.

Erik took in Samuel's round, olive face, his portly stomach, the little round glasses perched high atop his nose. He leaned toward Samuel, as if to smell his fear. Erik felt some dark, ancient instinct well up in him, the instinct to hunt. To root out. But the feeling dissipated just as suddenly, and he was left with Aviva, who had moved closer to Samuel, and was no longer looking at him with curious adoration, but with open-faced fear. He watched as Aviva took her husband's hand.

Erik looked furtively around and saw his German comrades in the distance, leaning lazily against a truck, far out of ear shot and paying no attention. The French officers nearest to him remained intently focused on their own clipboards, on counting the loaves of hard bread, and determining the correct spelling of the names on their questionnaires. Erik looked back to Aviva and smiled.

"Of course," he said kindly. "Catholic."

A surge of relief coursed through Aviva and Samuel, a relief so physically strong that it caused Ora to stir in her arms. Samuel tried to catch Aviva's eye, but she remained locked on Erik as he filled out their questionnaire. She watched him purse his lips as his pen moved across the sheet of paper that had the bare facts and lies of her life printed on it. Instead of feeling afraid that any of her lies would be found out, she could only wonder what this German soldier's mouth felt like. Then she wondered what his mouth would feel like on top of hers. Then she willed him to stop writing and to look up at her, to see her.

Erik looked back up at Aviva and Samuel. "And your address?" he asked.

Samuel started to answer, but Aviva cut him off.

"I live at 54 rue de Pasteur," she said. She stared at Erik with an intensity she hadn't known it was possible to feel. He returned her gaze, and an electric current seemed to pass between them. It was as if they were the only two people in the word; there was no Samuel, no Ora, no lines. She nodded toward her street in the distance, but didn't taker her eyes from his. "Right down there."

~

Aviva closed her journal and gazed up at the ceiling. Footsteps crept across her head in the apartment above her, and she wondered what her upstairs neighbor was doing awake so late. Perhaps the old man had his ear to the ground, and was listening to her, wondering what *she* was doing. Or maybe he was fumbling with his own choices in the dark, the way she was.

At the other end of the table she noticed that Samuel had left out the train and boat tickets. Why was Sam always doing that, leaving things out that should be hidden? Maybe for her to find them. Were they meant to be small reminders for her, a reminder that they were bound together, that his destiny was also hers and Ora's? What made him think she needed to be reminded of that? Perhaps he knew more of her secrets than she realized.

She picked up the tickets and studied them: a train to Marseille, a ship to Shanghai, one stop in Tokyo. This journey, that journey. This man, that man. One choice.

She opened up the hidden compartment in the

table, and the wood squeaked loudly against itself, breaking the silence. She paused, held her breath, and listened: Samuel and Ora did not stir; the footsteps above her did not resume. She put the tickets inside of the table, then slowly lowered the wooden block back into place, careful not to make a sound.

She didn't want to make this choice. She wanted someone else to choose for her.

She studied the photo. She turned it over. On the blank side, she wrote their names: *Samuel, Aviva, & Ora Druker, 1941*. She tucked the photo into the front page of the journal, placed the journal at the center of table—a book that held every thought she'd had, every feeling she'd felt, every action she'd taken over the past two years—and went back to bed.

Let Samuel find it, she thought, lying in bed next to him, still unable to sleep. Let Sam find it, and let him make this choice for her.

5

The next day, several things were supposed to happen: She and Ora were supposed to leave with Erik that evening. But first, Samuel was supposed to find her journal lying in plain sight on the table, read her it, understand that she'd been dishonest and disloyal, and tell her that she was worse than the teenaged whores flirting with Germans in the street. And then either banish her from their home, or forgive her. If Sam chose forgiveness then she, Samuel, and Ora would leave the house immediately, in case Erik came there looking for her, and make their way to Marseille a day earlier than expected, the three of them. If Sam chose banishment, she would wrap Ora up and go to the meeting place that Erik had decided on and wait for him to arrive. Then they'd make their way to Switzerland, the three of *them*.

But when she finally woke up, she could feel that it was already late morning. The space beside her where Samuel had lain was cold, his side of their shared blanket neatly smoothed and tucked into the mattress. A man who didn't trust his wife with something as simple as making up his side of the bed.

She found him in the kitchen. Samuel was spooning a bowl of milk into Ora's mouth, something he'd loved doing since Aviva's small breasts had dried up. She looked for her journal on the table, but there was only Ora's bowl, a glass of water, Samuel's newspaper.

"You slept late," said Samuel, his way of greeting her.

"I was up late," she said, her brain still not fully awake. "I was thinking about…" She searched for the words, but they were trapped in the grogginess of her mind.

"About what?" he asked, rather blandly, as if their entire lived weren't about to change forever. He continued feeding Ora and glanced at his newspaper. He hadn't read her journal, it was obvious.

"About this journey," she said. Her mind was starting to clear. "To Shanghai. About this choice."

Samuel put his newspaper down. Ora tried to

reach for the spoon sitting in the bowl of milk, but she wasn't strong enough yet, and her hand simply grabbed at the air.

"Remember, Aviva," he said. "There is no choice."

Samuel stood and began to clean up breakfast, still holding Ora. He was a good man, a capable father who took care of his child. Did they even need her?

Aviva looked into the living room and saw that it was emptier than yesterday. Almost all of the luggage that had been there was now gone. Her red trunk was nowhere to be found.

"Where are our things?" she asked Samuel.

He kept moving around the kitchen. "Everything is overbooked. We're only allowed one suitcase per family on the train." He calmly readied his briefcase for work, still talking to her. "But I was able to send our things ahead, early this morning. You were still sleeping."

As she stood speechless, he pulled a folded piece of paper from his pocket and showed it to her: *Seymour Synagogue, The Synagogue of Shanghai*, and an address written below. "There's already thousands of Jews there, maybe tens of thousands," he continued. "They'll help us when we arrive."

He handed Ora to her and returned to the kitchen

to place the address in the hidden compartment. He didn't see the frantic look creeping onto his wife's face.

With Ora in her arms, Aviva couldn't pace the room the way she wanted. She wanted to open every closet. She wanted to look between the cushions of their sofa. She wanted to check every drawer.

"My journal, the one I write in," she started, trying and failing to keep a note of panic from entering her voice. "And my mother's valise. Where is it?" she asked,

"Your book?" He finally stopped moving around, and looked at her thoughtfully. "I must've packed it with your other things. Inside your trunk. Why? Was it so important?" he asked, but didn't wait for an answer. "Anyways, just the necessities. Everything else will be waiting for us when we get to Shanghai."

Was he toying with her? Had he read it, or hadn't he? Did he know, or did he not know? Perhaps he'd read the journal, and then purposefully packed it up and shipped it away. Perhaps this was his way of forgiving her, pretending not to know of her crime and then hiding the evidence.

Samuel picked up his briefcase and headed for the door.

"I must open the bookshop as usual," he said.

"We don't want anyone to know we're leaving until we're already gone."

She wanted to protest: Let's leave now, right now. But then she realized that this was what it's like when other people chose for you. You want them to take control, and then they do, but that leaves you with no power, and you just accept that. Don't you?

~

All day, Aviva roamed the house aimlessly. She thought of Laurienne. In the afternoon she sat outside on the steps and gazed at the building across the street, expecting Laurienne or Gus or their son to emerge at any moment. But they didn't, of course. They were gone.

She wondered if any of her neighbors would be out lingering in small groups, discussing what had happened the night before. Laurienne had given birth to her son at home, and some of these people had been there, had seen the small, wailing creature take his first breath. But if any of their neighbors were mourning Laurienne, it was in the privacy of their own homes. The streets were far emptier than normal. Now that Laurienne had been killed and Gus arrested, his pamphlets found, their quiet neighborhood would be labeled a hotbed of enemies of the Reich. Any tears shed for Laurienne would be further proof that every single person on rue de Pasteur was a member of Free

France and was plotting with the Resistance to overthrow the Vichy regime. Better to shed no tears at all, and ignore Laurienne's blood still staining their street.

An image of Laurienne's wild face flashed through Aviva's mind: Laurienne ran away from the police, Laurienne ran away from her husband and from her son. She saw her friend fall to the ground again and again, shot while trying to flee.

Aviva knew what she must do. She had to tell Erik that she could not flee with him, that she could not choose him over her own family. She must tell him that there was no choice.

By evening, she had formulated a plan. Erik had said they'd meet after dinner, so that no one would question his absence until the following morning. She was supposed to give Samuel some excuse, then come and meet Erik. He'd told her not to bring any bags with her because it would raise Samuel's suspicions. Erik would have everything they need.

So, after Samuel came home from work, after they ate their bland dinner in soft silence, she said the words that she had practiced with Erik.

"I've been inside all day," she said to her husband, handing Ora to him. "I think I'll go out for a quick walk."

Samuel simply nodded. "Be careful," he told her absently, his mind perhaps already in Marseille, already in Tokyo, already in Shanghai. Where was the primal side of him, she wondered, that sniffed out competition and fought with snarled teeth for what was rightfully his? He had no gut feeling, no fire in his belly telling him to tell her not to go. She supposed that some men simply didn't have it, and that she'd gotten one of those men. She shook the thoughts from her head, those old, familiar feelings of dissatisfaction. If she shook them from her mind often enough, they would drop away from her like stones, and she would refuse to pick them up again.

As she stepped outside and closed the door, she could hear Ora as she giggled and gurgled in her father's arms. For a split second, Aviva panicked. Maybe she should stay home, maybe she shouldn't go to meet Erik at all. She was already an hour late; maybe he'd already given up on her. But she knew he hadn't. If she didn't show up as planned, Erik would come looking for her. He would come to their home, he would confront Samuel. She knew he would. And Samuel would lose. She knew he would.

And besides, she owed Erik this. An apology, an explanation. A goodbye.

6

It was just after twilight, and darkness was closing in. The building where Erik had told her to meet him was only a few blocks away from her own, but the street it was on seemed abandoned, every window of every building boarded up. No street lamps, no light anywhere. Deserted.

As she made her way toward the end of the empty street, she wondered if Erik was hiding in one of these buildings, watching her, wondering why Ora wasn't with her, guessing at her impending betrayal. But Samuel was her husband. *He* was the one she'd betrayed. Erik was a young man. He could go to Switzerland without her. She and Ora would only weigh him down, hadn't he thought of that? They'd be a burden to him. This what she'd tell him.

Aviva was walking as slowly as she could and practicing her speech when Erik suddenly sprang out from around the corner. He was in plain civilian clothes, a look of wild freedom all over his face. He had managed to slip out of the military barracks undetected; he had escaped the dungeon. Now he was ready to rescue the princess from the tower. But why did she look like that? Why did she look like she was about to tell him something he did not want to hear?

"There you are, finally," he said. "I've been waiting for almost—"

"I know," she said quietly. "I'm sorry." She tried to remember the speech, but the words were lost to her. Something about weight, something about burdens. She was sorry, so very sorry. But she was still only thinking, not speaking out loud.

"We have to leave now, Aviva," Erik said in a rush, not wanting to waste a moment of their new lives together. Something was missing, though. Something made no sense. "Ora?" he asked. "Where's Ora?"

The question was innocent and ludicrous. Wasn't it obvious? The three of them were supposed to be escaping together, but she had come alone. Did Aviva really have to spell it out for him? It angered her, that he was going to make her explain what should have already been painfully clear.

"Erik," she started, "I can't." She forced herself to look him in the eye. "I can't go with you."

There was always a precipice to understanding, a line that must be crossed between ignorance and knowing. Would he choose to cross the line on his own, or must she drag him?

"You can't go tonight?" he asked. His face shone naively in the darkness. "Why not?"

Aviva drew a breath. She would have to drag him.

"I mean, I *won't* go with you," she said. "I have to stay with my family." Then she added, "With my husband."

She watched for any change in Erik's face, in his body, in his breath. But he only stared blankly at her. His silence gave her courage and she went on, rather stupidly setting aside her script and replacing it with an excess of truth.

"You see, we're going to Shanghai, it's all arranged, Samuel's done it," said Aviva, as if she were chatting with Laurienne. "And I have to make a choice, and really—"

Suddenly Erik grabbed her by the shoulders. He said nothing, but his grip slowly tightened as he stared at her silently. She fought back the urge to whimper and squirm, instead looking at him squarely in the face as she continued.

"I have to make a choice," she repeated quietly. "And there *is* no choice."

Suddenly, he let go of her. He turned away from her, and stared at their empty surroundings as she studied him, her mind racing ahead to what she hoped would be the end. Was this it? Could it really be so easy? Please, let it be.

But no. He started pacing in front of her, blocking her from the street so that she felt pinned against the building behind them as he screamed into the night air.

"Do you have any idea," he said in a low growl, "of the risks I took tonight?" He stopped pacing and put both hands against the wall on either side of her head, trapping her even more. His reddening face hovered over hers. "My *life*, Aviva," he hissed. "My *life*."

He snatched himself away from her and resumed pacing, and she tried to calculate the space between them, wondering if there was enough room to slip past him as he pivoted back and forth.

"I've left my barracks," he continued, his voice climbing. "I can't go back now!"

It was the first time she'd ever seen him afraid, and it made her afraid because she couldn't predict what it meant for him. She knew what Samuel was like when he was afraid: skittish, indecisive, deferential. She knew what *she* was like she was afraid. But what would Erik be like? She didn't know.

He finally stopped moving and stared in the distance, his face red and twisted in a mix of fear and rage. She took the opportunity to slide out of her prison between him and the building wall, and steps out onto the street. Space, here. Freedom. But her movement shakes him from his fearful reverie, and he grabbed her again.

"No," he said, his voice icy now. "This won't happen. You're coming with me." Erik took her by the wrist and started pulling her down the street, away from her neighborhood. Deeper into the darkness.

A voice popped into her head. Was it hers, or was it Laurienne's?

Run, the voice said. *Run for your life.*

She waited for his grip on her to slacken, and when it did, she wrenched away from him and ran. She ran toward light. She ran toward noise, voices, the sound of cars and feet on pavement. She looked back only once, and saw that the feet on pavement were Erik's feet, chasing her.

She hadn't run like this since she was a child, the line between terror and exhilaration too thin to perceive. She felt a sharp pain in her side, and she fought to fill her lungs with air. She could hear Erik behind her, closing in, his long quick strides would soon overtake her. Just when she seemed to hear the creak of his elbow as his arm extended to grab her, people emerged. A street lamp. An open shop. A bored policeman looking with only half-interest as she and Erik ran past him. Light from windows. There was light.

She pushed through the clots of people mulling in the street. She could hear Erik slowing down behind her as he realized where she was headed: home.

As she approached the corner that would lead to her street, the pain in her side was becoming unbearable. But she told herself to keep lifting her legs, to keep breathing. She saw Samuel sitting at the kitchen table, rocking Ora to sleep, looking vaguely annoyed with her for having gone out after dark. He would want to go over their escape plan once more: train to Marseille in the morning, then a boat to Shanghai the next day. Then that would be the end, nothing more after that. There was no later life to imagine, just getting to Shanghai was everything, was enough.

She rounded the corner, expecting her street to

still be as quiet and bare as when she'd left it. Instead she found a crowd of people, all fixated on some scene ahead that she could not see. She recognized no one. She tried to push through them toward her home, but the wall of people was inflexible, unmoving. She glanced back and saw Erik standing at the corner, leering from the shadows. He was keeping his distance, and she tried to tell herself that his fear made her safe, that he had too much to lose to risk being discovered here, out of uniform. Home was just a half a block away. She just needed to get there.

She pushed ahead, squeezing herself into every tiny space she could find, slowly making her way to the front of the crowd. A police car, a Gretel, came into view. It was parked in front of her building. A single officer stood next to it at attention.

She started to recognize the faces of her neighbors. One gasped when he saw her. Another turned his head away. Another, an old man who lived above Laurienne, openly gaped at her.

"What's happening?" she whispered in his direction. But he didn't answer.

Everyone—her neighbors, the strangers, the single officer—was watching her building door, and so did she. She felt her throat close. She wanted to be confused, but somehow she wasn't. Somehow she knew.

Half a moment passed, then Samuel — led by one policeman and followed by another — came outside with Ora clutched to his chest.

She watched as Sam followed meekly behind the leading officer, and thought that Erik must have done this. But he couldn't have. Because here was Erik creeping up behind her, the crowd parting more easily for his tall, strong body. She glanced back as he pressed into her, and she could see the look of confusion and fear still etched into his face. He didn't know what was happening, either. This wasn't his doing. Then whose?

Just as Samuel was about to climb into the police car, a gripping hand from the policeman guiding him in, he looked up and saw Aviva standing at the edge of the crowd. They locked eyes. But Samuel did not allow his face to show one glimmer of recognition towards his wife. With some fleeting form of telepathy that they had never shared before, his eyes sent her a single message comprised of a single word that told her everything: *tallit*.

Aviva imagined it all in a flash. The antique dealer, who had pretended to believe the tallit was just a rug, had turned them in. While she had been with Erik, Samuel was being interrogated, and then arrested. *Not for being a Jew*, the policeman would've said, *but for lying on the official census about being a Jew*. She could see the conversation that must have occurred in her absence: Sam sweating beneath the intimidating glare of the officers, looking anxiously at Ora sleeping in her crib, looking anxiously at the door waiting for Aviva to return, praying that she wouldn't return, that at least his young, innocent wife could remain free.

Then, he and Ora were gone. Seated deep into the darkness of the Gretel. Then, the Gretel drove away.

The crowd remained still, as if they were frozen, their feet glued to the road. None of her neighbors would look at her, and she wasn't sure if they were trying to protect her, or themselves. Perhaps both.

This was the new state of local loyalty. No one would have stepped forward and pointed her out to the officers. No one would've said, *There she is, she's his wife, she's one of the ones you came for. Don't forget her, take her, too.* Her neighbors would not blatantly offer her head to the guillotine. But neither would they save her, neither would they rescue her. Nor would they explain to her what exactly had happened, why the officers had come, why her husband and daughter — a child, only a baby — were being taken away. Because that would require speaking to her, and they would not. Could not. There'd been two arrests on their street in two days. Now, there could only be safety in silence.

Why hadn't she stepped forward? Why hadn't she turned herself in, gone with them. They should all be together, no matter their fate. But in that moment when she and Samuel locked eyes, it wasn't only him she saw. She saw Laurienne running wildly away from the police, away from her own family, and the blood spreading across the front of her dress as she tumbled forward. And while Samuel was sending her the message about the tallit, she was receiving her own message from Laurienne: *don't move. Don't move forward, don't move backward. Remain completely still, and it will all be over soon. Don't make the same mistake I did. Save your own life, by doing nothing.*

Suddenly there was another voice in her ear.

"This was meant to happen," Erik was whispering. "Don't you see? You're meant to be with me."

Aviva slowly turned around to face him. The crowd finally began to look at her more directly, wondering what she would do next, where she would go now, and who was that blond man she was speaking to, didn't he look familiar to them in some dangerous way?

She knew they were watching, but she didn't care. There was a shame welling up inside her, and with it, rage.

"What?" she asked him coldly, keeping her voice low so that those standing nearby could not hear. "What did you say?"

Erik noticed the people now staring at him, studying his face, and his own fears crept back in.

"We have to get out of here," he said. He grabbed her arm, and started pulling her away from the crowd.

Suddenly, a noisy Hansel came rumbling down their street, a big German truck with a Nazi flag waving from its roof and an attached spotlight illuminating the road, the buildings, the crowd. In the back of the open truck stood a German soldier with a megaphone, screaming into it in horribly accented French that it was now curfew and that anyone found outside after curfew would be shot. The Hansel barreled toward the crowd, and it soon became clear to everyone that it had no intention of stopping.

Everyone moved at once. Erik, panicked at the sight of the German soldiers, tried simultaneously to duck out of their view and to grab Aviva, but she easily slipped free of him, moving away with the crowd down the street as he searched desperately for an alley, a shadow, anything to hide himself from his compatriots. But there was nowhere to hide. If they saw him, and recognized him, here in civilian clothes among French citizens on a street now known as a den of partisans and Jews, he would be the next one arrested. He would be next in the shooting line.

Aviva knew this too, and melted in with a clump of people crossing the street, in full view of the Hansel and its soldiers. Like a zombie, she moved forward with the crowd, letting it surge around her and push her forward. She did not look back to see if Erik was behind her. She'd seen the look of terror on his face. She knew that he was a deserter, and that when the choice came down to pursing her or saving himself, he would choose himself. She let herself be moved away from her home, not knowing where she was going, a zombie moving with the crowd. A walking dead.

7

As midnight approached, Aviva sat on the cold ground in an alley several blocks away from rue de Pasteur, her back against a large metal trash bin. She wanted to go home, perhaps it was safe now. But could Erik be waiting for her there? No, he wouldn't risk that, not now. He knew it was over. And the police might come back tomorrow or in a few days, looking for her.

Unless.

Maybe Samuel had concocted some elaborate story to discourage them from looking for her, telling the police that she had run off days or weeks earlier with another man, the whore. It wouldn't be far from the truth. The policemen would feel bad for him, a cuckhold, a single father taking care of a small child, no dignity or freedom left. Perhaps they'd give him extra bread and milk, a softer bed, out of pity.

And what if they did come back, and found her there? They'd arrest her, too, and she would finally be back where she belonged, with her family.

After another hour, once the air was totally quiet of footsteps and engines and voices, she pulled herself up and walked home.

The door was unlocked. The front room was in shambles: seat cushions ripped open, the drapes pulled down and wadded in a ball in the corner. Had the policemen done this, or had looters come later, hearing about an empty apartment? Did a neighbor do it?

Ora's crib was smashed to pieces. The police must have done it, to scare Samuel into submission. They should've seen in the curve of his back that he already was submissive.

What would they do with Ora? She'd heard horror stories of what the Germans did to Jewish babies. But these weren't German officers, they were French. And it wasn't a crime to be Jewish. Not yet. Even as she thought this, she knew that their existence was a crime, even if the Nazis and the Vichy regime were still figuring out how to make it so.

Inside her now empty home, Aviva sank to the

floor. For several minutes, she sobbed softly, freely. She stopped at the sound of a car—a Hansel? A Gretel?—rolling down the street. With the drapes torn down and the windows bare, the car's headlights shined brightly into the apartment, illuminating Aviva curled up on the floor, frozen. Once the car passed and the light faded, she breathed again.

She moved into the kitchen and found the cupboard doors ripped off. She looked at the kitchen table; the table cloth was wadded into a ball on the floor, but the table itself was surprisingly intact. A jolt of hope pierced her.

She moved her hand slowly to the hidden compartment, taking time to convinced herself that surely the police would have found this, it would've been the first place they looked. Slowly, she lifted the loose panel of wood, knowing in her heart that it would be empty.

It wasn't. Inside lay her husband's kippah, and beneath that several papers. She pulled them out one by one: train tickets to Marseilles, boat tickets to Shanghai, the address of the synagogue. She put the kippah back inside the compartment and closed it.

The kitchen chairs had been busted up and looked like pieces of kindling scattered around the floor. So instead of sitting down, Aviva sank to her knees, lay her head on the table, and wept tears of gratitude for the husband she had never been able to love, and would never see again.

Part 2: Mr. Chen's Restaurant & Café

November 1941, Shanghai

8

In the kitchen of Mr. Chen's Restaurant & Café — nestled in a charming brick-and-ivy building on a busy corner of the International Settlement of Shanghai — Chen stood at the counter reading and rereading a letter from Japan that told him that his wife, who had been missing for one year, was coming home.

He should have been chopping vegetables. Behind him his three kitchen maids, who he called Auntie One, Auntie Two, and Auntie Three — based on seniority — were busy scrubbing the floor, stirring soup, and flattening dough. He could feel their puzzled eyes on his back, unaccustomed to him standing still, apparently doing nothing. Normally he moved briskly through the restaurant, always finding a task to set himself on, to set an example for the staff and for his young son, Little Tao. Through the windows of the swinging doors he could see the dining room filling up with customers for breakfast. He should have been working.

But again he read the date on the letter, fuzzy now from having been read and reread, unfolded and refolded. The letter had arrived one week ago, and said clearly and simply: his wife, Su, would arrive on a ship from Tokyo, and he must be at the docks to meet her on the day and hour of said arrival in order for her to be *released*. The letter seemed formal, almost bureaucratic. He didn't know who had written it, or what was meant by "released." But he knew that the day was today, and the hour was now. And that his wife had finally come home.

He had only shown Tao the letter that morning. For the past week, Chen had kept it hidden under the bed in the room they slept in over the kitchen. A year ago, he wouldn't have been able to hide anything from Little Tao, so curious and energetic was the boy, so intelligent at only seven years old. But when Su disappeared, it was as if every spark of curiosity and interest in life was drained from Tao. From Chen, too.

Now, Little Tao was standing on his father's feet, trying to grab the letter out of his hands. Chen playfully swatted him away.

"Go on, Tao," said Chen. "You'd better get ready."

Tao just stared at him and at the letter in his hands. Chen had naively thought that his son would be delighted with the news of his mother's return, that the year of her absence would melt away instantaneously. When Su first disappeared, Tao had sat in the dining room in front of the large windows that looked out on the street. As days bled into weeks, Tao spoke less and less, until Chen realized his son had stopped speaking entirely. No longer brimming with energy and noise, the boy's eyes and ears seemed larger from months of silently watching and listening to the adults around him, taking everything in and keeping it, like a sponge holding water.

"Come on," Chen urged, "we don't want your mother to think we've gotten her."

Finally, something like a smile showed on Little Tao's lips. Chen wished he would speak. But maybe the boy was saving his words for his mother.

As he helped Tao into his jacket, Chen caught two of the kitchen maids exchanging a knowing look between them. They looked up and saw him staring, but he quickly turned away and guided Tao out of the kitchen into the dining room. He didn't know want to know what they thought of Su, or of him. It didn't matter anymore.

As soon as Chen and Tao left the kitchen, One and Two descended into gossip, never breaking from the work in front of them.

"I suppose she's finally back from her Tokyo Tryst," said One, feveringly scrubbing the floor on her knees with a soapy, hardwire brush. Bubbles popped around her head. "I guess being a whore for the Japanese wasn't so great after all."

"I heard she was *taken*," said Two, picking up the vegetables that her boss had left un-chopped. "Some big-man captain saw her out walking at the market and just...*took* her."

Auntie One opened the back door to dump her pail of dirty water into the alley. "Well, even so," said One, "did she put up a fight? Leaving her son, her husband like that."

Auntie Two dashed her knife expertly across a bulb of garlic. "I heard that she—"

But she was interrupted by Three, who slammed her hands into the dough that she'd been kneading, sending a puff of flour into the air.

"Enough!" said Three. One and Two stared at her

as if she'd gone mad.

"Not even Mr. Chen knows why his wife disappeared," Three continued, calming slightly and putting her fingers back in the dough. "So I highly doubt you two half-wits know anything about it."

Auntie Two looked slightly ashamed, and turned her attention back to the garlic. But Auntie One was unmoved, one hand on her hip as she pointed her brush at Three.

"Well I suppose he'll get his answers today," Auntie One said grimly. She moved to a new spot on the other side of the kitchen, and started scrubbing with an air of defiance. "Won't he?"

Out in the dining room, Chen had stopped to give his headwaiter instructions for running the restaurant during his absence. Mr. Chen's Restaurant & Café, known affectionately by its guests as "Mr. Chen's," was a staple in Shanghai. His patrons were Chinese, American, British, Japanese, German, French; for every nationality that could be found in Shanghai, its citizens eventually found their way to Mr. Chen's. Any language you wished to learn could be picked up by taking a table at Mr. Chen's in the morning, and by evening you'd be fluent.

ather had opened the restaurant, wisely
es of foreigners that had begun
Shanghai as individual opportunities
arms. Shanghai was dubbed the Paris of
the ... d the city quickly became filled with
nightclubs and gambling rooms, and other darker
entertainments. But where could the British ladies go
for a light morning teatime, and where could a young
Russian man spend a heavy afternoon brooding over
Marx, while spooning into his sullen mouth a *borsch*
that tasted just like home?

Realizing that this was the sort of place that
was missing from the city fabric, the original Mr. Chen
sat down and handwrote a menu from his own
memory of dining weekly with an Italian silk merchant
to whom he delivered the bamboo spools on which the
silk was wound, and whose wife was French. He
remembered almost every dish from those evenings —
scuete fumade, duck a l'orange — and spent hours
teaching his son, the present Mr. Chen, how to say each
dish in it's native language and in English, and how to
cook it with the soul of its native country. If it wasn't
on the menu, just tell Mr. Chen — first his father, now
him — the name of the dish and a general idea of how it
should be prepared. You'd find it on the menu the next
time you came to dine.

But Mr. Chen's father hadn't lived to see a new,
more dangerous Shanghai. The Japanese had occupied

his city for over four years, but had largely left the International Settlement—where most of the foreigners lived and worked and played, and where his restaurant was located—alone. Even still, he'd felt the menu had to be perfectly balanced so that British foods did not seem more plentiful then German dishes; he'd had to add far more Japanese soups than should have been necessary. He'd added more Chinese food, too, his own patriotic wink to himself. The menu no longer made any culinary sense—his father would be appalled—but it was a gastronomical map of the current political situation in Shanghai: tense, unnerving, everything thrust together but nothing mixing properly.

Now, Chen was surveying his restaurant as he and Little Tao made their way to the door. Should he bring Su back here, or would that be too much for her, too many familiar, questioning faces? Shouldn't they be alone, for a few hours at least? There was so much to discuss. Perhaps he should have left Tao in the kitchen with the Aunties. But it was too late now.

A few customers nodded respectfully at Chen as he passed by their table, and an older American woman reached out to pinch Little Tao's cheek, but Tao batted her hand away with grown-up indifference.

At the door Tao stopped suddenly, causing his father to bump into him from behind, whose mind was already at the docks, already picturing the his wife's pretty, round face. He looked down and saw that Tao was staring at something across the restaurant, and Chen followed his son's gaze.

At a table in the center of the dining room sat a Japanese man, Lieutenant Kiyata, and some young German soldier who Chen did not know. Kiyata came to his restaurant frequently, and Chen had developed a comfortableness with the man that he did not ordinarily feel amongst his Japanese guests, especially the military ones. But Kiyata was always polite when his comrades were rude, always reserved when his friends were boisterous. The German soldier seated with him now was much younger than Kiyata, of a lower rank, small-bodied with a bright shock of white hair atop a weasely face. The German had grabbed the long black ponytail of his waitress, was now wrapping it around his hand, and gave it a playful yank. The waitress froze, not knowing what to do.

Kiyata seemed to be trying to ignore his dining companion's behavior. The Japan-Germany alliance was strong, and Chen knew that they often felt a need to force social relationships between the two countries' citizens where ones did not naturally exist. They didn't have a common enemy, per se, but they had common interests: Germany expected to rule all of Europe, and Japan expected to rule all of Asia. Same goal, and similar ways of achieving it.

Still, Chen understood that each man was only a man, with his own moral codes and ideals. He hoped that Kiyata would tell the young German soldier to stop; he'd been at this restaurant so many times, he should know better. But Kiyata was only watching with a look of detachment.

Chen made his way over to their table, Tao following closely behind.

"Enjoying the soup sir?" Chen said to the goofy-faced German. He quickly let go of the waitress's hair, and she scurried away gratefully. The German now avoided Chen's gaze, and focused on his soup.

Kiyata regarded Chen with cool control, unperturbed by his companion's actions, or by Chen's. He had a job to do, and he was always doing it, at all times. He smiled benignly up at Chen.

"Do you know why I love dining in the International Settlement, Mr. Chen?" said Kiyata. "There is the French Concession, the British and American Quarters." He gestured toward the man sitting with him. "Our dear friends, the Germans. All within a stone's throw away from each other."

A younger Japanese officer hastily entered the restaurant and approached Kiyata. While the officer whispered something in Kiyata's ear, Chen watched as his son clandestinely removed the Nazi pin from the

German soldier's jacket draped against the back of his chair.

Kiyata gave his officer an affirmative nod, and the young man dashed back out of the restaurant as Kiyata turned back to Chen with the same benign smile.

"It is the perfect place to hunt our enemies," he finished. With that, Kiyata gestured to the large open window that wrapped around the entire restaurant, giving the diners a clear view of the street. Chen followed Kiyata's gaze. He saw a young Chinese men wearing bifocals, walking with a stack of papers under his arm. Chen watched as Kiyata's officer and another Japanese soldier suddenly accosted the man, ripped his papers away, and pinned him to the ground.

Chen looked back to Kiyata to find his face full of smug satisfaction. An anger that had grown familiar to him since the occupation had begun welled up in him. But he plastered the same benign smile onto his own face that Kiyata was so good at.

"You'll find no enemies here," Chen said, drawing Little Tao back to his side. "Only the best food in Shanghai."

Chen put an arm around his son, and Lieutenant Kiyata watched them go.

He admired Mr. Chen, the dignified way with which he carried himself. Kiyata returned his attention to his dinner companion, but after taking in the German's dull expression, decided not to force the conversation with this young, silly boy. He hated these forced relationships with the Germans, he'd have rather spent the morning in his room writing a letter to his parents, extolling the virtues of the work he was doing in China. They were pacifists in the old Buddhist way, and didn't believe in the war. But he, Kiyata, did. At least, most of the time.

He put his spoon into his soup and drew it to his lips. As he opened his mouth, he looked down to find the German soldier's Nazi pin floating in the center of his spoon.

Walking away from the restaurant, away from pessimistic maids and Japanese lieutenants, Chen and Little Tao headed briskly to the docks, ready to welcome Su home.

9

The ship slowly approached the dock, already teeming with fishing boats. The passengers crowded onto the deck, some of them coming home, some of them seeing their new home for the first time. There were merchants traveling between Tokyo and Shanghai, bringing back Japanese snacks and comic books that the Japanese community would pay double their original price. There was a large small group of refugees from Europe, who'd boarded the ship on the coast of France. Some were Italians defecting from their military, some were Dutchman who refused to submit to Germany, some were Jews from the occupied territories. They kept to themselves mostly, all sitting together in the cafeteria during meals, not talking to each other, so much as mourning.

Every evening, one of the same three films from America was shown on the projector, and everyone aboard would use the film lines to practice their English. They would need it once they got to the International Settlement, where everyone spoke English in crisp, kingly accents, even the Russians. In the International Settlement of Shanghai, they'd heard that every country had it's own neighborhood, every European city it's own miniature version of itself. Little Vienna, Little Prague. It would be a place where they could feel at home, without the actual dangers that pervaded their actual homelands.

Aviva spent most of the ship's month-long journey in a room all to herself, with three beds, two of them remaining empty. She took scraps of paper from wherever she could find them, so that she could write. She missed her journal, the cathartic daily outpouring o f whatever ridiculous thoughts or treacherous actions she'd taken during the day. Samuel had packed it in her valise, and that luggage had probably never even left France. She imagined their belongings being stopped at the post office and confiscated after

Samuel's arrest. Some policeman had probably found her journal, and read it aloud to his comrades, laughing at the whimsically depressed thoughts of a woman-child.

On the scraps of paper she found, she wrote a single word over and over: forget. Forget the country where she used to live, forget the family that she used to have. Forget about Samuel, forget about Ora. She would create a new Self in a new country, and leave the old one behind with her guilt, with her shame, with her memory.

When it was time to disembark, Aviva remained on the deck after everyone else had left, gripping the railing until her knuckles turned white.

~

At the harbor docks, Chen and Little Tao stared down into the still, white face of Su, nestled into a cheap coffin.

A Japanese cabin boy stood next to it, trying to shove some documents at Chen to be signed so that he could get away from grief-stricken father and son. They were standing close enough to the ship to touch it, and the passengers had to move around them to disembark. But Chen barely saw them. He only saw Su.

"What happened?" Chen asked, his voice little more than a rasp.

"I don't know," the cabin boy said in whining voice. "He just told me to unload it, and to give it to whoever comes for it."

It. The body. His wife. Tao's mother.

Chen grabbed the cabin boy by his collar, and shook him until the boy cried out in pain.

"Who? Who told you?" asked Chen, his choked with rage.

"Tomoto," said the cabin boy, and pointed toward the ship. "It was Captain Tomoto."

Chen and Little Tao followed the cabin boy's shaky finger. Standing at the upper most deck of the ship was a man in a Japanese captain's uniform. He was staring down at the city of Shanghai as if he owned it, or as if he planned to.

But Chen didn't recognize the man. He turned back to the cabin boy for more information, when suddenly someone clamored into his wife's coffin. He looked down to find a redheaded girl sprawled at his feet, her clothes threadbare and her cheeks flushed.

Aviva had fallen directly onto a coffin, finding herself face-to-face with a dead woman. She wanted to stand up, but she could not. She wanted to pull herself away from the dead body, but her own body refused to move. She started to shake. She felt a gentle hand on her back, and looked up into the kind face of a Chinese man.

"Miss," he said. "Are you alright?"

Chen reached down again to help her up, but the girl quickly pulled away from him and fled into the crowd, and Chen turned back around to find that the cabin boy, too, had dashed off.

When he looked back at Su, he found his son bent over her body. Little Tao was shaking his mother, as if trying to wake her from a deep sleep.

Chen tried to pull his son away from the body, but Tao slapped at his hands angrily. He'd been silent during this entire time at the docks, shocked into an even deeper silence than he'd been in for the past year. But now he was a bull of fury, and started hitting his father on the stomach and kicking his legs. Chen grabbed his son, and pulled into an embrace, squeezing him tightly until the boy stopped struggling against him. Chen looked back up to the top deck of the ship, but the man, Captain Tomoto, who had sent his wife back to him in a box, was already gone.

10

Aviva stood on the sidewalk looking up at an imposing stone building, grand letters etched into a grand archway overhead: Seymour Synagogue.

It had taken her all morning to find it on her own, weaving through the maze of fish carts and vegetable stalls, every street sign in several languages, too many. Japanese soldiers were everywhere, and she watched as two of them tossed a bucket of steaming hot water onto a beautiful Chinese woman, for no apparent reason. Would be it be Paris all over again, the occupiers torturing the occupied, simply because they could? Had she only left one besieged city and exchanged it for another? She had. After walking a few miles and unsure of whether she was going toward the synagogue or away from it, she sat down in a pathetic heap and simply watched people pass her by.

But she had made it there now, and she willed herself to go inside. But what if the people here knew something about her? Who had Samuel spoken to? What if they asked about her family?

Aviva looked down and noticed there was a chalkboard sign leaning against the doorway. Written on it in child-like, friendly lettering was a single word: *Welcome*.

She pushed open the heavy doors, and went in. She followed a buzz of noise through several wide cavernous hallways, until she found herself in a large open room filled with at least a tired-looking hundred people, clearly recent refugees, some of them from her own ship. Besides the refugees were several busy-looking women in bright blue shirts giving instructions and passing out items. Aviva wondered if the women in blue shirts had once been refugees themselves, and had become volunteers, committed to maintaining a certain calm, organized chaos. There was a long line of people against the wall, waiting for soup. Her stomach rumbled.

She turned to find the end of the line, and found herself facing the large back of a rabbi, his beard so full that she could see it from behind. He was gesturing widely with his hands and speaking in a high, jovial voice, as if he wasn't surrounded by wretchedness, by hunger, by a wasteland of need.

"Food, clothing, blankets," the rabbi was saying to someone Aviva could not see. She leaned to one side and looked around the rabbi to find a young man, no older than her, holding a notebook but not writing in it, and looking slightly bored. The young man noticed Aviva looking at him, and perked to attention.

"Books for schools!" the rabbi continued. "Shanghai has opened its doors to us, but this country cannot provide for us while its own people are starving."

The rabbi realized that he no longer held the young man's attention. He turned around to see who had stolen it, and beamed when he saw Aviva standing there.

"Welcome, my child," he said, so loudly that Aviva felt embarrassed. "Tell me, what is your name?"

"Aviva," she said quietly, biting back the instinct to say her last name, 'Druker.'

The rabbi did not seem to notice her discomfort, and complimented her, again too loudly, for having such a beautiful name. He introduced himself as Rabbi Mesner.

The young man next to him stepped forward and thrust his hand out to Aviva.

"Mick Ryan," he said. "Newspaperman, at your service."

Even before he started talking, she somehow sensed he was American. Something about his boyish, expectant face, the openness of his gaze, a halo of blind optimism surrounded him.

Mick said he was doing a story on the synagogue for his American newspaper. Rabbi Mesner hoped that if ordinary citizens saw how dire the situation, they'd donate money to the synagogue for the refugees.

"In fact," said Mick, eyeing her, "you might make a good cover story. A girl all alone in a foreign land, escaping the terrors of war." He made it sound like some kind of film, sad but glamorous, where everything was all tied up neatly by the end.

"Can I interview you sometime?" Mick asked her.

Aviva did not have to think some quick response to put him off, because she found herself being pushed aside from behind. She turned to find a large group of Japanese military men, all staring seriously at Rabbi Mesner.

The rabbi spread his arms generously and welcomed the men in the same manner he had with Aviva, though it was clear even to her that the soldiers were not there to reciprocate his warmth.

"Lieutenant Kiyata, so good to see you!" said the rabbi. He eyed the cadre of grim-looking soldiers, maintaining his easy smile. "And I see you've brought some friends?"

~

While Aviva was taking her first steps in the city of Shanghai, Chen had been slowly navigating his way from the docks toward the graveyard. The wooden casket was so cheap and thin, Su's body so light inside, that he could have carried it himself. He would have liked that. That intensity of effort, that focus of putting one foot in front of the other for miles, the weight of wood and a dead woman on his back, similar in weight to the grief in his heart.

But Tao was still with him. His son was quiet again; the angry little fists that had pounded his father's legs were now still. Tao's silence had never really bothered him before, but now this adult-like somberness unnerved him. Chen wanted to be alone with Su, to touch her cold skin—*Had they kept her in an icebox all the way from Tokyo? Yes, of course they had*—to kiss her blue lips. He thought of hailing a rickshaw and sending his son back to the restaurant alone, but he immediately saw the selfishness of such an act. They should be together, all of them. So instead he stopped a teenaged boy he recognized, the son of an acquaintance, and asked him to run as quickly as he could to the restaurant and deliver a message to his staff. After that, he did finally hail a rickshaw, though two empty ones passed him by after noticing the long wooden box at his feet.

The puller was older then Chen, at least 40, and gracefully helped Tao into the seat before telling Chen to get on so that he could lay the coffin horizontally across father and son. The puller didn't ask who was in the box, he didn't even ask where they were going. Because the Japanese had already begun to fill mass graves with Chinese bodies—no coffins, no ceremonies, no prayers—and so anyone lucky enough to have a box, thin and cheap as it was, must be going to the last remaining cemetery of Shanghai. The gratitude he felt for the puller mixed strangely with his grief, and with his confusion over the mystery man, Captain Tomoto, who was somehow responsible for this. His head was pounding, so Chen closed his eyes, and let the rickshaw rock him and Tao, and Su. He hoped they would never arrive at where they were going.

Now Chen and Tao watched as Su was lowered into a shallow grave at the foot of the hilly green cemetery by the sweating gravedigger.

Behind them stood the three kitchen maids in a

row. Nearby was another funeral party, much larger and very loud, clearly burying someone highly respected as they went through the usual elaborate custom of ringing gongs, chanting prayers, and burning money. But Chen only held a few sticks of smoking incense, as that was all that the cemetery director would give him. The director had said Chen was lucky to even receive a grave space at such short notice, but Chen knew the real truth. No one dared say it to his face, but there was a righteous indignation that permeated certain corners of Shanghai over his willingness to serve Japanese military men and Kempei officers at his restaurant. So when his wife disappeared, Chen and Su became the subject of gossip rather than sympathy, most assuming that she'd willingly run off with someone to Tokyo. The teenager he'd sent to the restaurant with the message of his wife's death must have told others—his father, his father's friends, who told their friends—and the fire of pleasure at his loss was quickly spreading across the city, flames of satisfaction and indignation.

    The simplicity of his wife's service was now a clear reflection of his Su's low position. Auntie Two and Auntie Three accepted their incense sticks from Chen with sympathetic faces. But Auntie One, stone-faced, refused hers with a simple wave of her hand. Chen was too weak to react, even to this obvious slight. He returned to his place in front of the coffin, while One tried hard to avoid Tao's sorrowful, reproachful gaze directed at her. Chen, Tao, Two, and Three all bowed their heads slightly as the gravedigger finished up, and after a moment, so did One.

Just as the coffin had been lowered all the way down into the ground, a decrepit old woman from the nearby funeral party hobbled over and began to shriek at the bowed heads of the kitchen maids.

"Why do you bow to her?" the old woman said shrilly, the fine jewelry at her neck and on her fingers gleaming in the sunlight. "That whore for the Japanese!"

The old woman then directed her screams directly at Su's grave.

"I know who you are!" she said. "I know what you did!" She lifted her intricately carved cane toward the grave as if she intended to poke at Su's body with it. Chen faintly recognized the old woman, one of Shanghai's rich widows, probably burying her brother or one of her many sons. But still he could not muster up any reaction, remaining rooted to the ground.

To everyone's surprise, it was Auntie One who sprang into action.

"Oh go away, you old goat!" she said, shooing the old woman. "They'll be ringing gongs for you soon enough."

The woman was taken aback by the kitchen maid's brassiness, clearly accustomed to the humility of servants, and quickly returned to her own group, all the while maintaining an air of reproach.

Chen looked gratefully at One, but she avoided his eyes as she took her place behind him again.

The gravedigger leaned in seal the coffin lid. Chen, Tao, and the kitchen maids all did an about-face in unison, turning their bodies away from the coffin according to custom, so that Su's soul could rest in peace.

"It's done," said the gravedigger.

Chen and Tao turned back around and moved closer to the grave as the man began shoveling dirt onto the coffin. The kitchen maids linked arms and departed the cemetery to return to work, leaving Chen and Tao there alone.

"*Ba*," said Tao. Dad.

Chen looked down in surprise at the simple sound his child had finally uttered. He waited for more sound to emerge. But when they came, he was unprepared.

"What is a whore?" Tao asked softly.

Chen sometimes forgot that choosing not to speak did not mean choosing not to listen, that Tao heard everything, perhaps more than Chen himself even heard. He silently hated himself for allowing the old woman to say that word in front of his son, and allowing his son to see him do nothing to stop it. What must the boy think of him?

Chen kneeled down so that he was eye-level with his son.

"It's nothing," he said. "just just what they call a woman when she makes a mistake."

Tao considered this with the seriousness of an anthropologist studying social rituals in the bush.

Then he asked, "What did Ma do?"

Chen rose and looked at Su's grave, slowly filling with dirt, her coffin almost completely covered now.

"Remember when your pet cricket died," said Chen, "and you asked me why, and I told you that I didn't know?" He kneeled back down to his son. "Well, this time, I'll find out. I'm going to find out why your mother died," he said. "I promise you."

The gravedigger finished filling the hole and plopped down on the soft ground near Su's grave in exhaustion. He wiped the sweat from his forehead with a rag, unmoved by the grief-filled vows that he heard every day. Promises that he knew would not raise the dead, no matter how much the living thought they could.

11

Aviva stood uncomfortably between Rabbi Mesner and the soldiers, but no one told her to move, so she remained still, her eyes bouncing back and forth between them.

"We're here about certain unfortunate rumors," said Kiyata.

The rabbi looked confused. "Rumors," he repeated. "What rumors?"

Kiyata gave a knowing smile to the rabbi's glibness, but otherwise ignored it.

"The rumor that some of your people are,

perhaps, unsympathetic to our cause in Shanghai." He stared hard at the rabbi. "And that some of your refugees may even be *involved* with supporting a local resistance movement?"

Rabbi Mesner exclaimed that he knew nothing of this, then to Aviva's surprise, turned to her. "Aviva, my dear, have you ever heard of such a rumor?"

Aviva stammered a denial. She felt like she was in a play, where everyone knew their lines but her. The rabbi turned to Mick, who had been unabashedly enjoying the show unfolding before him.

"Mr. Ryan, have you heard this rumor?"

Mick grinned, holding up his hands in joking surrender. "Hey! I'm just an impartial American here, guys."

Kiyata looked disdainfully at Mick. "*Impartial*," he repeated slowly. "What an interesting choice of words." Now he turned to Aviva. "Miss, do you believe that men can remain impartial in times of war?" he asked her. The crew of soldiers behind him were all staring at her.

"Perhaps men can't," she said, looking at Kiyata, "but women often must."

Mick laughed out loud, and even the lieutenant seemed amused by her.

Kiyata returned his attention back to the rabbi, all business again. "I hope I've made my point, Sir," he said. "Do not forget that your people are only allowed into Shanghai by the grace of our benevolent emperor."

The rabbi looked around at the refugees that had been moving meekly around them, lethargic from malnutrition, shivering in their thin clothes.

"I assure you, Lieutenant Kiyata," said Rabbi Mesner, the exuberance suddenly gone from his voice. "These people will never forget why they are in Shanghai."

Kiyata nodded curtly, then turned on his heels and left, his officers following quickly behind like a line of ducks following their mother.

The rabbi turned to Mick. "I'm afraid that I must cut this interview short, Mr. Ryan."

But Mick was busy scribbling furiously into his notepad. Mick Ryan had come to Shanghai to cover the Japanese incursion into this huge, sprawling country, but so far his assignments had been relegated to local business openings and closings, the occasional consulate gala. He had pitched this article to his editor just to receive of a reprieve from what he'd been doing. But he didn't really care about the refugees. He craved intrigued, drama. He wanted to be in the thick of things. This lieutenant, Kiyata, seemed like he might be worth talking to. Mick was young but considered himself to be wise beyond his twenty-three years, and was sure that he'd ben sensing a shifting in Shanghai, and especially in the International Settlement. The Japanese presence inside the boundary had grown, there was talk of arrests by Japanese police in the European quarters, something that would have been unheard of even a month ago, and impossible just last year. Maybe he could catch up with this Kiyata guy. Maybe he could get him to talk.

"Oh, that's alright, rabbi," said Mick, already making his way back toward the door. To Aviva said, "I'll come back later for that interview," and then winked at her in the exact she figured an American boy would. Then he was gone.

As soon as Mick was out of earshot, the rabbi leaned in to Aviva with urgency, and spoke in a low voice.

"My dear, would you be so kind as to help me?" he asked. "I'm afraid I must ask something of you, and demand that you speak of it to no one."

Aviva felt surprised that a man like him could need from someone like her; that a man like him would have secrets. Of course she would help.

"We must move quickly," he said, and immediately started down the hallway, beckoning for

Aviva to follow. They climbed twenty or so steps to the second floor. She struggled to keep up with him as he spoke to her over his shoulder.

"Where are you from, dear Aviva?" She told him Paris, already too breathless from the effort of climbing the steps on an empty stomach, forgetting to lie to him and claim a different city as her home.

"Ah, things are not so easy there now," said the rabbi.

"Better than most, " said Aviva.

He looked approvingly at her. "That's true. I'm glad you understand that." Now they had arrived to the door of his study. "Now, I hope that you can understand this," he said, and beckoned her in.

The rabbi's office was simple; only a desk, a few chairs, and a large bookcase decorated the room. Aviva watched in confusion as the portly rabbi went over to the bookshelf, placed his hands underneath, and began to lift.

"Please," he said, his face already turning red. "Help me."

She went to him and positioned herself on the other side of the bookcase. The rabbi made three soft grunts, as if to say *one, two, three*, then together the lifted the heavy bookcase less than an inch off the ground and slid it slid it over less than meter.

"That's enough," he said, and they both gasped for breath. Then, the rabbi knocks on the wall, and the wall opened from the other side. Inside, Aviva could see a dark, rather shallow crawl space, and sitting on the floor was a young Chinese man. The man immediately stood, alarmed but composed, with the air of an intelligent gladiator.

"Wen Li," said the rabbi. "You must hurry."

"What's happened?" Wen Li asked.

Rabbi Mesner quickly explained the visit from the Japanese soldiers, and Aviva quickly realized that the rumors they'd been so concerned with were true.

"I'll leave through the courtyard," said Wen Li, already picking up a satchel and stepping out of the crawlspace into the office. He glanced at Aviva briefly, thanked the rabbi, and was gone.

Aviva felt as if she'd been dropped into the eye of a tornado, a swirling mess of soldiers and reporters and hideouts.

But the rabbi returned to his normal state of gregariousness at remarkable speed. He clapped his hands together and turned to Aviva and asked brightly, "Now, my dear, what can I do for you"

"Who was that man?" she asked

The rabbi considered her questions thoughtfully. "Wen Li is a man who will do remarkable things for his country," he said. Then added, "If he can only live long enough."

Aviva thought Gus and Laurienne, Gus's pamphlets, so committed to freeing France from the Germans that he was willing to risk his own life, and Laurienne's. Had she left behind that underground war, only to find it here, as well? She had.

"You have helped me greatly," Rabbi Mesner was saying. "Now, let me help you. Tell me what you need. Anything at all."

Now that the tornado around her had calmed, she felt herself plummeting back to the earth as her awareness her situation returned to her.

"I need everything," she said. "I have nothing." She suddenly felt a deep urge to talk. "I have no money," she said. "No clothes." She knew that she was talking herself deeper into despair, but she couldn't stop. "I don't know where anything is. I need work, but I don't know what I can do. I don't know who would hire me."

"Do not worry my child," said the rabbi, "you have come to the right place." He went to his desk. *"We* will feed you, *we* will clothe you. It won't be much, but it'll be something."

Aviva sat down in the chair across from him desk, almost collapsing in relief. This was what Samuel had said it would be like; that they would be taken care of here, that every thing would be alright. She hadn't believed him, then. But she believed him now.

"I already have an idea for a job for you, and you can even live there," the rabbi said.

She would have a job. She couldn't believe it. The only work she'd ever done was in someone else's home: cooking and cleaning from a young age to earn her keep with her cousin, then doing the same for Samuel. She'd never woken up with somewhere else to go.

"But tonight," the rabbi went on, "you will stay here. We've built living quarters!" he said proudly. "They're crowded, but clean."

"I don't want to take space away from anyone else," she replied. When she got off the ship, she had already assumed she would be spending her first night on the street, sleeping outside. It was cold, but she'd been cold before. She had shoes. Some of the other refugees she's seen did not have shoes.

"It's all right," said the rabbi, assuring her.

"Families are much harder to help. Finding a place to sleep for four, five, six people. Almost impossible. They end up living here, at the synagogue. But finding a place for one, a job for one young woman alone. Easy. Honestly, it feels good to do something easy right now."

Rabbi Mesner studied her, as if seeing the strangeness of her circumstances for the first time.

"But where is your family, my child?" he asked. "Who's child are you?"

It was the question she had been dreading from the moment she stepped off the boat. She drew into herself, as if she wanted to shrink from the kindly man's innocent prodding. When she finally answered him, she was unable to look him in the face.

"I'm no one's child," she said, looking down at her hands. "I was an orphan, and then the war began, and then Paris fell, and then they began ordering the arrests of Jews, and then I came here." She paused, then finally added, "I've been alone for a long time."

The rabbi came around to her and wrapped Aviva up into an awkward bear hug.

"So many of us are alone now," he said, patting her on the back.

Aviva quickly pulled herself from the rabbi's

arms, then stood up and awkwardly paced the small room. But there was nowhere to hide herself. The rabbi was watching her with quiet patience, but to her it felt like she was being appraised. She stopped pacing and faced him.

"Aren't you afraid of those men, those Japanese soldiers?" she asked. "My boat stopped in Tokyo, and a whole slew of them got on. I saw them. It was like they were headed to battle."

Rabbi Mesner was replied calmly, as if he'd asked this same question to himself many times before.

"And if I were afraid?" he said. "What would I do with such fear? What would you do with that fear?"

Why did he keep turning the conversation back around on her? She started to pace again, frustrated.

"I don't know," she said, "Not antagonize them, not hide people here!" Her breath came fast and shallow, but she couldn't stop moving. "You would sacrifice your own safety for that man? That Wen Li?"

The rabbi regarded her in silence, then finally returned to his desk and leaned back in his chair. He remained quiet until Aviva stopped pacing.

"One is never closer to his true nature than when he has forgotten himself in the service of others," he said. "So I suppose the answer to your question is:

yes. I place Wen Li's well-being over my own." He paused and looked seriously at Aviva before continuing. "I do this to know who I truly am."

He scribbled a short letter while Aviva watched him petulantly, exhausted from her own efforts of deflection.

When he finished, she took the paper from him. Another paper, another address. Written at the top was the name of the place where she would start her new life, and she read the words softly aloud: *Mr. Chen's Restaurant & Café*.

~

Chen could not hear his name being whispered from deep inside the synagogue. He was on the other side of the International Settlement, carrying Tao home from the cemetery. They had lingered amongst the graves, noting which ones were fresh, like Su's. It was already dusk now and shops were closing up, employees rolling down the steel shutters over their storefronts and bakery owners removing pastries from display windows.

Chen had been carrying his son for miles, and the physical effort mixed with the emotional strain of the morning was bringing him close to tears. Finally he stumbled, almost dropping Tao. He put the boy down and started walking again, but Tao refused to move.

"*Ba*," said Tao. "Carry me."

"You're too big now," he said, and started walking again. "I can't carry you and myself too."

He looked back and saw that Tao still had not moved, so Chen stopped and stretched out an arm to his son, an offer to hold his hand.

Tao ran toward his father, but to Chen's surprised, the boy passed him and kept going

Tao ran through the street exuberantly, every step taking him further and further from his mother's grave, her blue-white body, her face that should have been smiling at him but remained still. He didn't look back to see where is father was, not once. Soon he arrived at a thick circle of people, and stopped. He could hear voices arguing loudly, but tall adult bodies blocked his view.

Tao pushed his way through them to the center of the circle, and found a Japanese soldier holding a severely drunk Russian woman by one arm, while a British Foreign Police officer held her by the other as she squirmed between them. She wore a silvery dress that was slightly soiled and hung so low that Tao could see the tops of her bosom. Bright red lipstick was smeared down her chin. He'd seen women like this hanging around outside his father's restaurant in the evenings, trying to talk with any male customers who had dined alone. But his father had always showed these women away.

"Need I remind you," the British policeman was saying, "that this is the *British Quarter* of the International Settlement, and only *British officers* are authorized to make arrests."

The crowd of onlookers grew behind Tao, but he couldn't stop staring at the beautiful woman. She must have felt his eyes on her, because she blinked several times and then focused in on him, grinning baldly down at him.

"Your British street is in Shanghai," said the Japanese soldier, "and in Shanghai, the *Emperor* decides who has what authorization!"

Suddenly the Russian woman wrenched away from the soldier and the policeman, and gaily pitched herself forward, coming down directly on top of Tao.

"*Him*! I want to go with him!" she said in a thick accent laced with liquor, which Tao smelled as she pushed her face close to his. "It's my son, my little *lapochka*."

She clumsily wrapped her arms around Tao and cradled him, and he looked at her in happy, frozen awe.

Chen pushed his way to the front of the circle,

and shook his head in disbelief at what he saw there: it was his wife, Su, sitting on the ground with their little boy wrapped in her arms, singing softly in some foreign tongue.

Chen closed his eyes, then opened them again. Now he saw Tao, curled up in the arms of a prostitute.

Chen quickly pulled Tao off of her. At the same time, the Japanese soldier yanked the woman roughly up from the ground and began dragging her away as she yelled out in pain.

Tao wrenched away from Chen, ran up behind the soldier, and pushed him from behind. The soldier turned around, and was immediately greeted with a kick to the shins from Tao.

The soldier threw the Russian woman to the ground, and grabbed Tao by the shirt. Chen rushed forward and took hold of his son by the arm. Both men, Chen and the Japanese soldier, tightly kept their grip on the child.

"You little rat!" the soldier said to Tao, ignoring Chen. "You dare strike me?"

The crowd that had circled the soldier, the officer, and the prostitute were now circling the soldier, Chen, and Tao. Chen hurriedly explained to the soldier that they'd just come from his wife's funeral and the boy was just upset by the loss of his mother. He tried to keep any note of pleading out of his voice, but he knew that if it became necessary, he would plead. He would for his son.

But now the Japanese soldier was looking more closely at Tao, as if he was just now realizing how young the boy was. Then the soldier glanced around at the mixed crowd—Chinese, British, Dutch—all glaring down on him, and he sensed the possibility of public defeat at the hands of a mob.

"A dead mother, eh?" the soldier said to Tao while releasing the boy's shirt from his grip. He stood and fixed his uniform, while Chen hugged Tao gratefully to his chest.

Then, as the soldier walked off, the crowd parting for him only grudgingly, he said over his shoulder, "What's one more dead Chinese woman?"

Chen watched him go, his face red with helpless rage. His grip tightened around the small, fragile body of his son, the only thing that was still his, that still mattered.

Instead of watching the soldier slink away, Little Tao was watching the Russian prostitute. She was still lying on the ground where the Japanese soldier had thrown her, now forgotten by both the soldier and the British officer. The crowd dispersed around her, and she closed her eyes, her face peaceful as she blissfully enjoyed a moment of well-earned rest.

~

Later that night, Aviva was lying down in the cramped sleeping hall that had been thrown up in the courtyard of the synagogue to house the refugees. She and several others had makeshift pallets on the floor, while older women slept in rows of beds. Some were sound asleep while others tossed and turned near her, murmuring fretfully in their sleep as if they were trapped in a nightmare.

She didn't mind sleeping on the ground, actually. She'd done it for years when she lived with Cousin Ruby. She remembered the day Ruby told her that she, Aviva, was getting married. She was Aviva's mother's cousin, forty years old and rather dour, unmarried and childless.

Every day she came home from work and sat in a chair at the kitchen table with her feet propped up on another chair, as if she only knew how to do two things, work and rest, work and rest.

One day she came home and instead of resting, Ruby pulled something out of the back of a closet and handed it to her young cousin. It was her mother's valise. She would need it, Ruby said to Aviva, when she moved into her new husband Samuel Druker's home. Just a week later she and Samuel were standing under a *chuppa* together, getting married. After the wedding Samuel stood around with the men drinking coffee and discussing Poland, and Aviva stood with the women eating cake and discussing Poland. She wasn't actually listening, though. She kept stealing glances at her new husband, wondering what they would do when they found themselves alone together, without anyone else around to talk to or stand with, except each other.

At the end of the wedding reception Aviva pulled Cousin Ruby away from the other women and said that she changed her mind, that she didn't want a husband, that she wasn't ready for this. But her cousin had turned away from, and began to clean up, and told Aviva that she would be glad she had a husband once the Germans were at her door.

12

The next morning, Aviva found it difficult to wake up, Cousin Ruby's dour face and harsh warnings still sweeping around her mind.

When she finally did get up, the other refugees in her room were already gathering up their pallets. She could smell food in the air, and she wondered if the line for breakfast was already too long. She remembered she that she had somewhere else to go, while the families who had woken up beside her did not.

She went to the rabbi's office to say goodbye, and to thank him. Volunteers were shuffling in and out, and the room looked different than the day before. Less bare. She realized there were stacks and stacks of suitcases now lining the wall where the bookcase had been, where Wen Li had hidden.

"Our missing persons," the rabbi said when he saw her staring at the stacks. "The ships, the trains, they're all crowded with people fleeing from Europe. So people send their things ahead." More volunteers filed in, carrying more suitcases. "And sometimes their luggage arrives, but they never do. Sometimes it means the worst. But not always."

Aviva was staring at one of the stacks. There were ten suitcases piled on top of each other. In the very center of the stack was a trunk painted deep red, with white flowers . Her mother's. Her own.

She didn't realize that she'd been slowly moving toward the stack of suitcases until the rabbi called out to her from behind. She turned to face him, and hoped that nothing showed on her face.

"My dear, you should go now, yes?" Rabbi Mesner said. "Your new life awaits you."

~

As Aviva was stepping out of the synagogue into the stark morning light and starting her journey toward Mr. Chen's—toward a new job, a new home— men were doing darker work a few miles north in a tiny cell in the basement of Bridge House.

Up the eastern bank of the Huangpu River,

north of the International Settlement past Suzhou Creek, was Little Tokyo, what the Japanese military men and traders and their wives have claimed as their home away from home. Bridge House was there, a large art deco building the Kempeitai used for their Shanghai headquarters, appropriated from a local landlord. Little Tokyo afforded them their own saki parlors for drinking, geisha houses for entertainment, a kaido primary school to educate their children, their own temples to whisper their own prayers.

Whispers. That was what Captain Tomoto sought. He'd woken up that morning before the sun had even begun to shine into his room on the top floor Bridge House, had only been back in Shanghai for less than twenty-four hours, and already he felt himself hungry for the hunt.

He'd been sent back to this city to root out whoever was leading some underground wave of freedom fighters. The war would soon expand from Japan beyond their Asian neighbors, new enemies were cropping up across oceans, and Shanghai needed to be a firm, reliable base for the Imperial Army. Anyone who threatened that must be terminated. Shanghai had belonged to Japan for years already, but still, there were embers of resistance that needed to be snuffed out.

Tomoto almost respected them, the way the

Chinese people protected one another, the networks of cellars and crawlspaces they kept reserved for any underground fighter who needed it. Sharing food while they themselves went hungry, believing it was for a greater cause. And in a way, it was better that they hid from him. If they didn't run, how could he chase?

But Shanghai felt different now. It was nothing like the first time he came in the 30's, when jazz music was roaring in the streets and the Shanghainese were brimming with a joy and exuberance that he'd looked forward to crushing. He'd made several trips since then, back and forth between Shanghai and Tokyo, a quarter of his life spent on ships, half of his life spent in battle. Then there was that final, small quarter of life that was just for him. That was time he spent with women.

He loved women, in a way that most people simply couldn't understand. He had a new girl waiting for him back in Tokyo, a Japanese one this time, as he'd recently lost his taste for Chinese women after the last one had spent an entire year wailing and crying for her husband, for her son, not an ounce of appreciation for the luxuries he showered on her, taking her into his own home, in his own homeland, an honor. Even after her death, he'd done her the dignity of bringing her back to Shanghai to be buried amongst her own people. A wasted effort, perhaps. Though it did give him the chance to see the husband and son at the docks, both of them looking down at the body like little lambs whose mother had been ripped open by a wolf. So that was the little family she'd been wailing about all that time?

Tomoto pushed those thoughts from his mind, and returned his focus to the task at hand. The sooner he finished this job in Shanghai, the sooner he could return home to Tokyo, to that sweet quarter of life where he invented games, made up rules as he went along, and whatever woman he was playing with had to learn them as quickly as possible, or risk the physical pain of his disappointment.

Now, he was standing at the doorway of a dark, dank cell in the basement of Bridge House. Sitting on the floor and chained to the wall inside was his prisoner, a local man arrested the day before by his lieutenant, Kiyata. Tomoto had been going at him for an hour, since the sun came up, and the man was bloody and damp with sweat, his head hanging down in defeat. Tomoto had given him a short break, and now the break was over.

The prisoner trembled as Tomoto approached him slowly, deliberately. He sat down in the chair that he'd placed directly in front of the prisoner, so close that the man could not avoid breathing heavily on Tomoto's shiny black shoes, fogging them up.

"Do you have any idea," asked Tomoto, as if they were old friends, "how happy I was in Japan?"

He looked expectantly at the prisoner as if he truly wanted an answer. But the man remained quiet, as if he knew that opening his mouth will only lead to more pain. So Tomoto answered for him.

"Very happy," he said. He leaned forward into the prisoner's face and whispered confidingly, "I woke up and made love to a different girl every morning before practicing *bujutsu* in my garden."

Still, the prisoner said nothing, carefully watching his tormentor. Tomoto stood and leisurely paced the room as he continued.

"But then I am called back to Shanghai," he said, "ripped from paradise because of the childish plans of scum like you."

Tomoto stopped pacing at the sound of footsteps behind him, and turned to find Liutenant Kiyata at the cell doorway, saluting him and carrying what looked like a magazine, it's sheets loose.

Tomoto takes it, barely glancing at Kiyata, then crouched down in front of the prisoner so that they were eye-to-eye. He placed the magazine under his own nose so that it was just inches from the other man's face, and told him to look at it. It was mostly illustration, a picture depicting hundreds of Chinese peasants fighting defiantly against a small Japanese militia, the Rising Sun flag burning, a symbol of Japan in flames. But inside the magazine was a long, detailed treatise on how the citizens must defeat the illegal occupiers. What made it so bad was the fact that somehow, copies were being distributed in Japan. Students mostly, or old religious folk who believed that everyone must be either monk or samurai or farmer. Still, it was an embarrassment to the Emperor, to have anti-Japanese sentiments being read within their own borders. And it was a personal embarrassment to him, Tomoto, because the magazine was dated during the last time he was in Shanghai. On his territory, on his watch.

"Are you the author of this...coloring book?" said Tomoto.

The prisoner looked over to Kiyata, as if for help or guidance. But Kiyata kept his eyes on a blank space on the wall ahead of him, still standing at attention because Tomoto had not given him permission to do otherwise. His father and mother lived in Nagasaki, where they ran a small orphanage for the children of dead soldiers. They were pacifists and had raised him to be one, too. But when his parents were jailed for speaking out against their nation's military conquests, considered a crime against the Emperor, it was Kiyata who got them released. He was a smart young man who was good at earning the loyalty of superiors. He joined the military that his parents had campaigned against, and quickly rose up in the ranks, and eventually petitioned for their freedom. Once freed, his father was too kind a man to outright disown his son, but still he seemed to disown him with eyes. Now his son was a Lieutenant, respected by his officers and well-liked by his superiors. Except for Tomoto, it sometimes seemed.

"It isn't mine," the prisoner was saying. "It was given to me."

Tomoto beamed at the man trembling before him and exclaimed, "A gift!" Then, ever so politely, he asked who the gift was from.

Perhaps it was the gaiety in Tomoto's exclamation or the false politeness in his voice, or something else, maybe the remembrance of a vow sworn amongst comrades. Whatever the reason, the prisoner suddenly drew a final ounce of strength from some hidden source, looked Tomoto in the eye, and told him that he couldn't remember.

Kiyata felt a wave of dismay, because he knew what would come next for the prisoner. Tomoto, though, looked pleased by the man's defiance, as if this was what he'd both expected and longed for.

"Well, then," said Tomoto, "allow me to help

you remember."

And with one sharp, sudden movement, Tomoto plunged his thumb into the prisoner's left eye. With his back to Kiyata, Tomoto could not see his lieutenant shutting his own eyes and grimacing against the screams of the man whose face he held in his hands, his thumb moving deeper and deeper. Tomoto could not even see the face of the prisoner. Instead, before him floated the faces of a dozen women, whom he had loved, in his own way. He remembered how he'd made them scream, each and every one of them, like seagulls screeching across the sea.

The prisoner was sobbing and writhing in pain on the floor, both hands over one wounded eye. Captain Tomoto watched him nonchalantly, and stretched out his own bloody hand to his lieutenant, Kiyata. But Kiyata's eyes were fixated on the prisoner, and something that looked suspiciously like sympathy was peaking through the lieutenant's face.

"Kiyata!" Tomoto said sharply.

Kiyata immediately returned to attention, straightening his body and returning his gaze to the blank space of the wall, willing the prisoner to stop writhing so that he could concentrate on pleasing his captain, on doing his job. Tomoto seemed to be waiting for something from him, but what?

"There's blood on my hands," said Tomoto.

As quickly as he could, Kiyata removed the white kerchief from his jacket pocket and handed it to the captain, who wiped his hands with it before tossing it back to Kiyata like a dish rag. After Kiyata refolded the kerchief and returned it to his pocket, he saw that the prisoner's blood had now rubbed off onto his own hands. He carefully hung his arms at his sides, careful not to touch his military uniform, not wanting the prisoner's blood to spread all over him.

Tomoto crouched back down in front of the Chinese man, who was now on his knees, one hand still over his eye.

"Do you remember his name now?" said Tomoto, patting the man's face gently with the little illustrated book of resistance propaganda that Kiyata's officers had found on him, the evidence that was the cause of his imprisonment, his present pain.

This time, the prisoner did not look to Kiyata, but instead stared up at the ceiling for several moments, as if searching for answers from heaven. He whispered something to himself: *May the ancestors forgive me*.

"What was that?" Tomoto almost screamed, grabbing the prisoner's collar. The time for games was over, he wanted answers now. "What did you say?"

The prisoner looked once more to Kiyata, then back to Tomoto, and Kiyata could tell by the shame and regret that was filling the prisoner's face that a name was coming, and that this moment would be over soon, for all of them.

The prisoner opened his mouth, coughed, then spat, then finally spoke. "His name is Wen Li."

~

At Mr. Chen's Restaurant and Café, Wen Li stepped into the kitchen from the alley door and was immediately greeted by a warm handshake from Chen, who quickly pulled Wen Li inside. Auntie One furtively peaked out into the alleyway to make sure no one was watching, then closed the door.

As Chen and Wen Li are sat down at the kitchen table, Chen took in the strength and determination that seemed to emanate from the young man's very being. He was seven or eight years younger than Chen, but taller, perhaps wiser, definitely more angry. Wen Li's father had had a history of kowtowing to the Japanese for favors. The old man was dead now — a heart attack in his sleep last year — but Wen

Li's anger remained. Chen, and almost every other Shanghainese man and woman who possessed even a hint of patriotism, knew that Wen Li was developing some sort of renewed resistance to the occupation, and they supported him however they could. A local dressmaker would design an expensive gown for a Japanese housewife, and then send a message through any of Wen Li's comrades to say that Officer So-and-So's wife was a big spender and was drowning her husband in debt, which may leave Officer So-and-So vulnerable to outside influence. A local butcher would sell his meat to the domestic servant of Japanese consulate administrators, but then send his oldest son to one of Wen Li's secret meetings to tell him the exact day and time the servants always came to market, leaving the administrator's home empty and vulnerable to anyone who might wish to look for documents that could expose any of the Emperor's current or future plans for Shanghai. The occupation had been going on for years, and outwardly many of the Shanghainese seemed to have given up. But still they wanted someone to continue fighting on their behalf. And someone was.

Now with Wen Li in front of him, Chen knew he should have been doing more to support their cause, more than just the bags of food he sent home with one of the Aunties every evening to dole out to Wen Li and his companions, wherever they were hiding.

"I'm very proud of you," Chen said to Wen Li.

"We all are," Auntie Three chimed in, pouring their guest a cup of tea and gazing admiringly down at him.

Wen Li gave a nod of humble thanks to the maid before turning his attention to Chen.

"I was sorry to learn about your wife," he said, with a look of such earnest condolence that Chen could hardly bare it. Chen turned in his chair and glanced around the kitchen for something to focus on, trying to avoid Wen Li's sympathy.

"Word travels fast in Shanghai," he said. He turned back to his friend and said lightly, "Sometimes it feels like a small village."

"It can, yes," said Wen Li. Then, he leaned in toward Chen and looked meaningfully into the older man's face. "Especially when we help each other out, the way villagers do."

Chen nodded understandingly. He promised that he would do whatever he could to help but that Wen Li must act more carefully now.

"There've been more arrests," said Chen. "It's hunting season in Shanghai."

Wen Li was about to reply when suddenly Tao

bounded down from the upstairs apartment, saw Wen Li, and pounced on him like a puppy. Wen Li hugged him back, and from his bag removed a small, wooden carving that looked like a miniature birdcage, inside of which sat a tiny lime cricket that now begin to chirp as if on command. Wen Li handed it to Tao, who gleefully accepted it from him. Chen savored every moment of this, knowing how little his son had smiled over the past year, thankful that such innocent happiness was not completely lost to the boy, especially now that they knew Su was gone forever.

"It is not only me and my comrades being hunted," Wen Li was saying to a distracted Chen. "It is the whole world they want."

Chen finally turned his attention from Tao back to Wen Li

"I need a place to stay," said Wen Li, his eyes staring directly into Chen's, almost challenging him. "Somewhere they won't look."

Immediately, Chen stood up, his chair falling backward and hitting the floor with a crash. The kitchen maids all glanced nervously at one another, then at the swinging door that led to the dining room, which was already full of early lunch customers.

"No," Chen protested. "My son is here! I cannot place him in any danger."

Wen Li stood too, undeterred, as if he'd expected this kind of objection. Tao was between them, looking up from one face to the other, the cricket crawling around in his cupped hands.

"He'll be in even more danger," said Wen Li, "if the Japanese take over the International Settlement."

Chen dismissed Wen Li's words with a wave of his hand, and said that that could never happen. But Wen Li persisted that it could.

"I hear that's why this captain has returned," said Wen Li. "This Tomoto."

At the sound of Tomoto's name, Chen turned abruptly away from his friend. He recalled the dark figure standing alone on the top deck of the ship. *Who told you?* he'd asked the cabin boy. Captain Tomoto. The same rage from the day before flared inside him like a sudden fire, and he could feel his face reddening. He turned away from all of them—Wen Li, Tao, the Aunties—and strode over to the swinging doors and pointed into the dining room.

"Look! Japanese come here almost every day to dine," he said to Wen Li. "It wouldn't be safe for you anyway."

Wen Li joined Chen at the doors, unafraid, and explained that *that* was what made this the perfect place.

"They won't look where they eat," Wen Li said with a confidence that Chen wished he felt.

Auntie Two nervously pulled Wen Li away from the doors to the far side of the kitchen, and Chen returned to the table and sat down, his mind heavy, his conscience throbbing like a sore thumb. Auntie One handed Wen Li a bowl of noodles—no doubt to make her opinion on the matter clear to her boss—and Wen Li ate it standing at the stove, giving Chen space to think, to lead himself to the right choice, the inevitable choice. A citizen could not hide in his kitchen forever. Wen Li knew that Chen knew this.

For several moments Chen watched Tao play on the floor with his new pet cricket, letting it jump over his finger and crawl across his small hands. He let his mind wander, to his father teaching him smatterings of English, Italian, and French as a child; to his pathetic additions of Shanghainese dishes to the otherwise European menu; to his son, who had looked at Wen Li with more admiration than he had ever looked at Chen.

Suddenly, Chen saw Su crouching next to Tao. She put her hand next to their son's, creating a bridge for the cricket to cross, and his wife and son were smiling as if it were the most normal of days. Then, Chen's eyes widened in amazement as Su rose and came over to him. He could feel the blanket of her long, loose hair hanging down and brushing against his arms as she leaned over him and began tapping him gently on the shoulder. He could not speak, but only gaze up at her.

In a far away voice, Su said to him, "Mr. Chen? Mr. Chen?"

He closed his eyes in disbelief. He could smell the sweetness of his wife's breath on his face.

When he opened his eyes again, he found himself staring into the pale face of a redheaded girl with large, brown eyes, who was tapping him gently on the shoulder.

"Mr. Chen?" Aviva said again. Could he see her, she wondered. Could he hear her?

Chen jumped up from his chair, bewildered, and Aviva quickly pulled away from him.

He was breathing heavily now, confused, and looked wildly around at the strange girl, the Aunties, Wen Li, and Little Tao, all of whom were staring at him. Had they seen Su, too? No. But they'd seen the look on his face, the way he'd breathed in some phantom musk, the way he'd jumped up from his chair like a wild man. Laughter and the clink of silverware came in from the dining room, and the familiar sounds grounded him. Finally Chen calmed himself, looked at Aviva. She looked familiar to him, somehow.

"Yes, who are you?" said Chen, not hostile, but still a bit breathless. "Why are you in my kitchen?"

Aviva glanced over at the kitchen maids, who did seem to regard her with slight hostility, an unknown woman in their little kingdom. She met Wen Li's eyes, and he nodded at her in recognition and gave her an encouraging smile.

She went to Chen, passing Tao but barely seeing him, not noticing how closely the boy watched her, a hint of affection already spreading on his face.

She handed Chen the letter from Rabbi Mesner, and studied his face as he read it. There was a sorrow that seemed etched onto the Chinese man's lips, so that even when he put the letter down and welcomed her with a smile, she could see something like grief behind it, pounding at the door of his heart, waiting to be let out.

~

Later that evening, while Wen Li was making a pallet for himself in the cellar of Chen's Restaurant and Café and the owner and his little son was showing Aviva her tiny room at the top of the stairs, Captain Tomoto and Lieutenant Kiyata walked the halls of the basement of Bridge House. The rows of cells were mostly empty now, but Tomoto said that soon they'd be filled.

"Have you ever heard of this man," Tomoto asked Kiyata. "This Wen Li?"

Kiyata shook his head, no. They rounded a corner, and walked smack into a young private who was dragging a huge, dark sack down the hallway. The private immediately released the edges of the sack to salute Tomoto, respect and fear on his face. Tomoto barely broke his stride and shoved the private out of his way with one sweep of his arm. It was not a hard shove, but the young private seemed to anticipate it and let himself falls away from Tomoto onto the sack he'd been dragging. From the top of the sack emerges the lifeless face of their prisoner, blood still caked around his eye.

Kiyata stopped to help the private back to his feet, then watched as the young man tried to push the prisoner's dead body fully back inside the sack, a puzzle of limbs that didn't seem to fit. Tomoto, sensing the emptiness next to him, also stopped and looked back, studying the face of his lieutenant for any hint of disloyalty or insubordination. There was something about Kiyata, a delicateness to the man that Tomoto did not fully trust.

"You will find this Wen Li," Tomoto said to

Kiyata. "Invite him for a visit. For a friendly chat."

Tomoto didn't wait for an answer from Kiyata before striding off, leaving his lieutenant behind.

Kiyata started after him, but looked back at the private, still heaving with effort as he inched down the hallway in the opposite direction, dragging the burdensome sack, one of the prisoner's lifeless arms trailing behind, knuckles gliding easily across the floor.

13

A week later, Aviva dragged a large trashcan across the kitchen toward the alley door, breathing heavily as the other kitchen maids eyed her, not offering help.

Mr. Chen had wanted her to stand at a podium near the door and greet the guests, lead them to their tables. But she preferred being in the back with him, the gentleness of his presence, the curious quietness of the little boy, even the mean grumbles of one of the aunties — was it One or Two? She couldn't remember. But she didn't mind them. What she wanted to avoid was the endless stream of faces coming through the front doors of the restaurant, the inevitable questions the European diners would inevitably pose: what's your name, where are your from, do you have any family? The three aunties called her Four, and to them she was from Outside Country, and maybe Fours from Outside didn't have families, so why bother asking? She even liked the smell of sweat rising from her body from morning to night, and the physical effort of loading and carrying and chopping somehow felt soulful to her. Not that she had any other work to compare it to, but still.

Aviva knew that it was silly, the way she romanticized working. But she remembered as a child asking Cousin Ruby if they could move to the countryside of France and live on a farm. She had promised she would do everything, milk the cows, fill the troughs at feeding time for the pigs. She wanted to hold something in her hands. Now she understood that she was being protected from this sort of labor. Cousin Ruby. What was she doing now? After she was married and out of her house, her cousin seemed to regard her as an acquaintance to whom she held no further obligations. She'd started to come around more once Ora was born, but soon the visits dropped off and they returned to the post-marital, pre-birth status quo. She and Samuel hadn't discussed what they would tell her cousin about their departure; there'd been no time to think of that. By now Ruby would have heard of Samuel's arrest, would wonder about the fate of her young cousin, who the woman had never even acknowledged was somewhat named after her.

Aviva gave the trash can one hard, firm push, and the can tipped over, rubbish spilling out across the kitchen floor. Only Auntie One laughed out loud, all schadenfreude.

"And when you finish there," said One to

Aviva with a smile, "I've got more for you to do."

Ahead of Aviva the basement door opened a crack, and Wen Li poked his head out into the kitchen, immediately followed by the head of Little Tao, the two doing a pantomime of bank robbers on the look out for a sheriff.

"All clear?" Wen Li asked Aviva, and she nodded. The two of them climbed the remaining stairs into the kitchen, and came over to her to help clean up the mess she'd made.

Aviva had to restrain herself from patting Little Tao on the head. He followed her around the restaurant silently as she cleaned, and hovered outside of the doorway to her tiny room, his figure outlined through the thin lace curtain Chen had helped her to hang for privacy. She had only seen glimpses of Wen Li over the past few days; there was a hidden door in the basement that led to a sewer, and Aviva supposed that he must creep through it after dark and vanish outside into the night. She wondered where he went, what he did, what was so important that he had to hide.

Now she and Wen Li watched as Tao picked something up out of the rubbish pile. It was an empty jar of rat poison, a skull and bones symbol plastered on the side, the clearest warning of death. Tao held up the can to study it, as if it were an interestingly-shaped rock to add to a collection.

"Careful," Wen Li said, taking the jar from Tao. "It's poison. It kills."

A waiter stepped over the trio on the floor to take a tray of food out to the dining room, and as the doors swung open they could see a loud, overcrowded table of Japanese and German soldiers, drinking and talking boisterously.

When the doors swung closed again, Aviva nodded toward the dining room and smiled slyly at Tao. "We'll use it to clear Shanghai of its rats," she said.

Wen Li and the aunties looked surprised and impressed by Aviva's sudden display of cheekiness, and Tao grinned up at her. Slowly, she thought, she'll become herself here.

Aviva finally managed the to pull the heavy trash bin out into the alley and set it down next to another. The other bin had no lid, and when she peered inside of it she found a long, heavy blanket, only slightly soiled but warm-looking. She pulled it out and looked up and down the alley, spotting a few doors with signs above them, one of which read in elegant script: *Zaolzie Fabrics*.

She hadn't been back to the synagogue since she'd

arrived at Mr. Chen's, had not even sent a note of thanks to the rabbi for finding her a place so quickly, so easily. She thought of the red suitcase that sat in his office. Had it been opened yet? She didn't know, and thought it was better to keep her distance. But she also remembered the weary faces of the refugees, the ones who'd been on her ship and the ones that were already crowding the synagogue when she first arrived. Would things be so quick and easy for them? Had they found their own place to live and to sleep, and was it warm enough during the cold November nights? She doubted it.

Inside the back office of Zaolzie Fabrics, Aviva stood before the desk of the shop's owner, an incredibly thin, sophisticated woman of Czech origin and middle age who slinkily smoked a long cigarette as she watched Aviva with some amusement. As Aviva explained what she wanted — to take the shop's damaged items and donate them to the synagogue; she would carry them there *herself*, she would clean them and patch them up *herself* — another woman with a short, square body and stern face worked methodically in the corner steaming large swaths of fabric, keeping her eyes on her work. The shop owner took a long, languid drag before answering Aviva in her fluid voice.

"I'm afraid it's really out of the question, darling," she said, and exhaled.

Aviva was undeterred, and held up the blanket she'd taken from the trash bin outside.

"But the synagogue needs blankets and clothing, and you're just throwing them away," she said.

With one thin hand, the shop owner waived Aviva's objections away like puffs of smoke.

"But you see, darling," she said, her voice almost a purr, secure unto itself, unmoved by the pleas of the redheaded French girl in front of her, "the Jews are enemies of the German state, which makes them enemies of the Japanese, though they don't say so." She gestured toward a row of gowns on mannequins, saying with a flourish, "And the Japanese are my best customers!"

The shop owner stood up and walked around her desk to drape one mantis-like arm around Aviva's shoulders in false intimacy.

"So you see, darling," she continued, "I cannot be known as a friend to the Jews of Shanghai. Europe may feel far away, but it is closer than you think."

With that she turned Aviva's body in the direction of the door, a ballet teacher guiding her pupil, and gave her a gentle push. "Now, Mrs. Borgrov here will show you out," she said, catching the steamer woman's eye behind Aviva's back and covertly pointing at the blanket still in Aviva's hands.

The steamer woman, Mrs. Borgrov, led Aviva back to the alley door, the way she'd come. Aviva tried to meet the woman's eyes; surely she had more empathy than her boss. But Mrs. Borgrov guilty avoided looking into Aviva's faces as she passed through the doorway back into the alley. Once outside, Aviva opened her mouth to make a final plea. But Mrs. Borgrov quickly snatched the blanket from her hands, and slammed the door shut in her face.

For several moments Aviva stood there, alone in the alleyway, blinking at the door. She wanted to pound on it with her fists. She wanted to light it afire. Suddenly, she thought of Laurienne who, if she were here, would say *Let's kick the door down. Let's take what we want.*

That night, Aviva took her frustration out on a dining room table, scrubbing it with intensity in the dark after closing time. The shop owner's smug face, Mrs. Borgrov snatching the blanket away. The table she worked on shone in the dark. She'd never felt so useful, and so useless, at the same time. She was so absorbed in her work that she didn't hear Chen come in from the kitchen.

"I think it's clean, Aviva," he said.

She threw the scrubber onto the table with an exhausted sigh. Chen pulled a chair over to her, and she collapses into it. He brought over a second chair for himself, but before he could sit down, she propped her feet up onto it and leaned back, closing her eyes. Chen looked at her, amused, then pulled up another chair and sat down.

"War does terrible things," he said in a ruminating tone. "Perhaps the worst thing it does is force beautiful girls to work who aren't so used to working."

Aviva opened one eye and pinned it on him, then closed it again. He was mocking her.

"I believe I'm a rather good worker, thank you," she replied, prim and proud.

Already, Chen was enjoying himself. He and Su used to do this, sit in the dining room in the dark after shutting down the kitchen, just talking.

"What did you do in Paris?" he asked. He trusted Rabbi Mesner, had known the man for years, and hadn't needed to question the background of the French girl he'd suddenly delivered into his kitchen. But still, he was curious.

Aviva put her feet back on the ground and sat up to look squarely at Chen. After only a week in this place, she felt stronger somehow. Further away from her home, from the past. She wouldn't let herself be dragged back there, even by kindly Mr. Chen.

"Tao's mother," she said. "Where is she?"

Now it was Chen who leaned back in his chair, and put his feet up where Aviva's had been. He'd finally realized where he'd seen the girl before: at the docks, her frightened face hovering so close to his wife's expressionless one, her red hair flying loose in the wind. But Aviva, apparently, had yet to recognize him.

"She left us," he answered matter-of-factly. "And then she came back in a box. On your ship, in fact."

Aviva's hands flew to her mouth. That was him. That was her.

"I'm sorry," she said. "How awful."

They sat in silence for a moment. Chen was strangely serene, while Aviva internally wrestled with what he'd just told her. She felt uneasy, as if she owed him something for his candidness.

"I left my family too," she said finally. "I was going back to them, but—" How could she make him understand? "They had already been...put in a box."

She hated her own words. She hated herself. She started to cry, silently at first, then began sobbing into her hands. She couldn't remember the last time she'd cried. Was it on the ship? No, she hadn't allowed herself that. It must have been the night Samuel and Ora were taken, when she was curled onto the floor of their empty apartment, scared and unsure of what to do next, shamed by her own survival. Chen put a hand on her shoulder, startling her. She suddenly realized what a risk she'd taken.

"Rabbi Mesner doesn't know," she said, voice thick with worry. "You mustn't tell him."

Chen looked into the girl's reddening face. He wondered, if Su had lived, would she have had to make such a pleading request to someone upon returning to Shanghai? *Please, don't tell my husband. He'll never forgive me.* But he would've forgiven her. He already had.

"A woman's secrets are hers to live with," he said, then stood up wearily and started to leave. But then he stopped, turned back.

Aviva looked up at him, bracing herself. She deserved his disdain, she deserved to be thrown out. Tell her she should be laying lifeless alongside his wife, two betrayers. Tell her the truth.

"But you must remember," he said, "that secrets cannot be kept for long. There is always evidence of our true selves somewhere."

He turned again to go, and Aviva watched his back as he said over his shoulder, "All it takes is for someone else to find it."

14

The next morning, Aviva Druker woke up with the remnants of a dream dancing across her mind: herself as six-year-old, red hair wild and tangled, and a blurred face that alternated between her mother's and her cousin Ruby's hovering over her as she opened a beautiful red trunk with cream-colored roses painted on it, finding a tattered book inside, somehow recognizing the handwriting but not understanding the words. Inside that book was a photo of two people and a baby, a family that the younger Aviva knew, but did not know how she knew.

The journal. Evidence of her true self. Eventually, someone else would find it. Unless she got it back first.

That afternoon, she went to the synagogue. She surprised herself by how well she knew the streets, as long as she remained inside of the International Settlement. Auntie Three, the nice one, had taken her around to the different shops to buy food and kitchen supplies, had taught her smatterings of Shanghainese, so that if she got lost and there were no Europeans or Indians around, she could comfortably stop a local person and ask for directions, though she couldn't guarantee she'd understand them. But her body somehow remembered the way there, as if a deeper part of herself had known from the moment she left for Mr. Chen's that her business with the synagogue was not yet complete.

When she arrived, the same friendly chalkboard sign welcomed her. In the main hall she was greeted by a crowd of refugees who seemed just as fresh from the docks as they'd been on her first day there. But she recognized a few families from that first day, and knew that while she had been easily placed, they would light be living in a broom closet in the synagogue for several months more, or forever, as the rabbi had said. They wore the same tattered clothing, while she wore a dress that was not exactly new, but it was new to her. She could feel a sense of hunger rising up from their bellies, and she cursed her full stomach and the easy, plentiful meals she ate with Tao in the kitchen of Mr. Chen's. She knew that one of the volunteers came to collected donations of food from

Mr. Chen every week, and that that was why Rabbi Mesner and Mr. Chen were such friends. She wished she'd thought to bring that week's donation with her, so as not to arrive empty-handed to the place that had found her a home.

She walked through the halls with such determination that an old woman assumed she was a volunteer, and stopped to ask her if she could possibly have an extra bowl of rice, just this once. Aviva cursed herself again; why hadn't she slipped something into the pocket of her dress to give away? An apple, or even a small piece of uncooked dough. Because there were only two things on her mind: a red valise, and inside of that, a faded old book with the handwriting of a stupid, young girl.

She stood at Rabbi Mesner's doorway and admired his bent, studious head as he poured over some papers at his desk. A dark-haired woman sat facing the rabbi. Aviva presumed she was a volunteer and could only see the woman's back, but there was an energy field around her of harsh efficiency and mild disapproval.

Aviva knocked. Rabbi Mesner looked up, and immediately stood, his arms stretched wide. It had been over a week since she'd seen him, and not even sent him a note of thanks for his help. But here he was right where she'd left him. Welcoming the prodigal daughter home.

"Aviva, my dear," he exclaimed. "Come in, come in! How are you getting along at Mr. Chen's?"

Aviva glanced at the corner of the room where the pile of luggage had been. It was still there, though looked like less of a pile now, each suitcase arranged neatly in stacks. She recognized her valise instantly, near the top of one of the stacks. It seemed, to her, to be glowing. How could the rabbi have sat here all these days and not noticed it? She turned her attention back to him.

"It's wonderful there," said Aviva gratefully. But before she could continue, the woman seated at the rabbi's desk suddenly whipped around, a short stack of white cards clutched tightly in her fist. Aviva and the woman silently locked eyes, and Aviva knew her immediately: it was the steamer woman from the fabric shop. What was her name? Mrs. Borschoff? What was she doing here? An intense wave of dislike emanated off the woman toward Aviva, and she turned back to the rabbi.

"They've been so kind to me," she continued, less effusive now with the steamer woman's harsh eyes on her. Aviva recalled the snatch of the blanket from her hands and the slammed door in her face. Borgrov, that was her name. She looked pointedly at the woman as she went on. "Not everyone has been."

Aviva was pleased to see Mrs. Borgrov's face immediately turn red. But the older woman would not be shamed so easily. She stood up from the rabbi's desk, her arms crossed.

"Lucky you," spat Mrs. Borgrov, "getting a place so quickly. I've seen some of these families here for months—"

Rabbi Mesner interrupted her.

"Mrs. Borgrov has been in Shanghai for many years. She leads the woman's groups and is one of our most dedicated volunteers," he said, placating Borgrov somewhat mechanically, as if he was used to the petty rivalries amongst his flock. "But never mind that. How can we help you?"

"Actually," said Aviva, a plan coming into view in her own mind, "I wanted to know how I could help you. I'd like to become a volunteer." She glanced at the luggage pile in the corner. "Perhaps I could help organize—"

"Volunteers are those of us who've been here a while," interrupted Mrs. Borgrov. "Who know how things work." She arms crossed her arms even tighter against her chest. "Don't need more bodies crowding in here."

Rabbi Mesner was looking between Aviva and the

older woman in hapless confusion, when suddenly a voice called out from the doorway, to which he responded with obvious relief.

"I was hoping I'd find you here!" said the buoyant, male voice.

Aviva turned to find Mick Ryan, the American reporter, looking directly at her. In one hand was a notepad, in the other a large camera. Mick beamed at Aviva, and Borgrov turned away from them back to her work, annoyed by the increase in attention toward this French girl who had seemed to come from nowhere, expecting special favors, following her around.

"Me?" said Aviva, more than a little confused.

"Ah, yes," said the rabbi. "Mick thinks you would make a perfect subject for his article about the synagogue."

Mick stepped into the office and set his notepad and camera on the top of the suitcase stacks that held Aviva's valise. He raised both hands into an imaginary frame around Aviva's face. "Tragically beautiful young girl crosses the treacherous seas all alone to escape persecution in Europe and finds a sanctuary in Shanghai," he said, as if he were reading a headline from a newsreel. "Now, *that*'ll sell papers.

The rabbi nodded enthusiastically. The synagogue was buckling under the weight of the latest influx of refugees, and new ships of them were arriving everyday from Europe. They needed donations, money. They needed people in places like America to care.

"And now she'll be one of our volunteers here as well," the rabbi said to Mick. Then turning to Aviva, he said, "What we really need, Aviva my dear, is someone to act as our official fundraiser."

The rabbi went on, but Aviva could hardly hear him. She was watching Mrs. Borgrov, who during this time had moved to the corner and had started attaching the notecards in her hand to the front side of the suitcases, moving stack by stack with quick efficiency, pointedly ignoring their conversation. Each notecard had a surname written in thick block letters: *Auerbach, Belenky, Czarniecki*. Aviva took a step toward Borgrov.

"What are you doing?" she asked, trying to keep the note of desperate alarm from her voice.

Borgrov replied with a look of exaggerated affront. "*Excuse* me?" she said. How dare this girl question her? She, who'd come to Shanghai with nothing, who proudly served the synagogue the same way she'd done in her Poland. So what if she didn't speak up when her boss spoke casually ill of Jews?

Was she supposed to tell everyone she met that she was one? Risk her job over a blanket? This wasn't Germany; she didn't have to wear a star. But she could see the judgment on the redheaded French girl's face. How dare she judge her, when it was she who volunteered here everyday, who just that morning had spoon fed a bowl of soup into the mouth of an old man while he whispered that he wish he had stayed in Poland to die there, instead of here with her.

Sensing trouble again, Rabbi Mesner quickly stepped in.

"We're just organizing the luggage with no apparent owners," he said to Aviva. "We look inside, to see what can be given to families in need. Shoes, clothing…" The rabbi's voice trailed off as Mick started tapping his pen against his notepad, looking childishly bored.

Rabbi Mesner pulled Aviva away from Mrs. Borgrov and the luggage, and the woman continued with her work.

"This is why I'd like your help raising funds," the rabbi said to Aviva, and she tried her best to focus on him. "I've the Japanese might be cutting off any incoming money from America soon."

At this, Mick perked up.

"Really?" he said. "Where'd you hear that?"

The rabbi smiled with air of a man used to avoiding unwanted questions. "A man doesn't have to be a journalist to have his sources," he said.

Mick suppressed an urge to press the topic. He needed a story for his editor or he'd be fired, shipped back to America and forced to stand on street corners selling penny papers like he'd done for years before they let him start writing. He'd convinced his bosses that he had the stuff of a major war correspondent, that he'd send them wires of revolution and political intrigue. But so far he'd written nothing. No one would talk to him, no one trusted him with any information that could be considered a scoop. Rabbi Mesner had let him in, but Mick didn't truly care about the synagogue in Shanghai and it's need for more money. He was Irish-Catholic, and the Jews he saw outside his apartment in Queens seemed to be doing just fine. He wanted a real story, a war story, a real scoop. If the rabbi wouldn't give him the information he needed, he'd find another way.

Mick said, "Alright, alright," waving off the rabbi's demurring with falsely affable chuckle. He arranged Aviva, who seemed to be in a bit of daze, next to Rabbi Mesner, and picked up his camera.

"Now, let's get a photo for Aviva's story," said Mick, to which Mrs. Borgrov replied under her breath as she kept arranging the cards, "*Her* story?"

As Mick fiddled with his camera, Aviva watched Mrs. Borgrov. The woman was standing directly in front of the stack with Aviva's little red trunk, working her way quickly down to it. A lump of dread seemed stuck in her throat. The rabbi put one arm around her shoulders and whispered for her to smile, so she did.

Mick said, "Over here, Aviva. Now one, two, three!"

Aviva watched as Mrs. Borgrov stuck a notecard onto the red valise. The writing was no larger than that of any of the other notecards, but to Aviva it seemed huge, like a neon sign over a theater. In clear block letters the notecard held a name, and a city.

Druker, Paris.

The light bulb flashed on Aviva's and Rabbi Mesner's smiling faces. His beaming, hers frozen in fear.

~

That evening, Captain Tomoto sat at his desk and watched with barely concealed contempt as Mick Ryan strolled around his office on the main floor of Bridge House like a tourist on the Seine.

Mick, for his part, tried to keep things light. He still couldn't believe he was here. He'd hounded Kiyata for weeks after meeting him at the synagogue, begging to be let in to Bridge House, where no reporter of any nationality had ever been allowed. He'd heard rumors of kidnappings, torture, all of it supposedly happening here, in this large building deep inside Little Tokyo. And now, here he was. He'd been escorted from the entrance door to the captain's office by two armed soldiers, and it had already been made clear to him that *this*—this little chat with Captain Tomoto inside his richly decorated office—was as far into the building that he would be allowed. Incredible though it was, he couldn't help but wonder: why let him in at all?

Now that he was here, Mitch wasn't sure how to begin. He admired the huge, heavy-looking sword that hung behind Tomoto over his desk. He stood near a tall bookshelf lined with what looked like a single series of a book broken up into dozens of volumes, Japanese characters he couldn't decipher in silver embossment down the spines. He thought of asking what the books were about, but decided against it. He strolled back to Tomoto's desk where he picked up a miniature carving of a girl drawing water from a well, looked it over with false interest, then set it back down. Tomoto gave a heavy, bored sigh, clearly losing patience.

"So," said Mick, "how long you guys been in this neighborhood?"

Tomoto rolled his eyes at the young man before him. He was tired of this city, of this country, and of the people in it. He had made more arrests, he had made more men bleed, but he had not yet found Wen Li. His superiors in Tokyo were busy planning their own excursions, and so no one was putting any pressure on him, besides himself. He hated failure, he hated distractions. And now here was this newspaperman with his Yankee accent, who Tomoto had thought might be useful, but who was really only wasting his time.

"Why are you here?" Tomoto asked.

Mick finally sat down at Tomoto's desk, all business now. "I'm more curious," he said, "about why you let me in here in the first place."

Tomoto considered thoughtfully before answering.

"I was curious," he said finally. "A *real, live American boy*." He gestured at Mick like a docent pointing out a painting in a museum. "I thought talking to you might be..." He trailed off, reaching for the correct English word.

"Fun?" offered Mick.

"No," said Tomoto, waving the idea away as if the notion were ridiculous.

Mick tried again. "Enlightening?"

"Definitely not," Tomoto said. Mick was about to make another guess when Tomoto cut him off.

"*Assuaging!*" he said suddenly, pleased with himself for finally recalling the word. He could see it printed in a schoolbook from twenty years ago, maybe longer. *To assuage one's guilt.* Not that he ever felt that particular emotion. But perhaps, ten years from now, when Japan ruled every island in the Pacific, perhaps he'll feel some twinge of guilt at the millions of dead bodies they will have buried in the sea in the name of the Emperor. And when that twinge of guilt comes, he'll only have to remember this moment, when this knuckleheaded American sat like a child before him, pestering him, annoying him, and any such guilt will be immediately assuaged.

Mick looked confused by Tomoto's choice of words, but quickly moved on, flipping open his notepad to a blank page.

"So," he said, "what are the Emperor's plans for Shanghai?"

At that, Tomoto threw his head back and roared with laughter, and Mick was so startled that he dropped his notepad.

"You see?" Tomoto exclaimed, still laughing heartily. He lifted his head toward the ceiling and stretched his arms wide as if Mick's presence were a gift from some amusing god. "*Americans!*"

Tomoto stood with a good-natured sigh, went to the bar and made himself a drink, leaving Mick sitting at his desk like a child waiting for a parent to return. This wasn't what Mick had expected, not at all. With Tomoto's back to him, he took in the room once more, and his eyes landed on a table against the wall, where an unrolled map was pinned down with various tiny figurines, all stalking toward a single location at the map's edge. Mick strained his eyes to decipher what region the map depicted, but Tomoto came back and handed him a glass of amber-colored liquor. In the coming days, Mick will remember this moment, because he will realize that the strange look on Tomoto's face was one of pity and knowing.

"Americans," Tomoto said again, and clinked his glass against Mick's. "You're always so busy looking around. You never look up, and you never look down."

Part 3:
Aviva & The Synagogue of Shanghai

December 1941, Shanghai

15

One week deep into December, Aviva was hosting a talent show at Mr. Chen's to raise funds for the synagogue, not knowing that thousands of miles away the world was about to change forever, and Shanghai with it.

A line of evening revelers stood outside the restaurant waiting to get in, and Little Tao sat on a stool at the door taking people's money and giving them tickets as they entered, bringing gay laughter and the brisk winter air inside with them. Next to him was the chalkboard sign that usually listed the day's special cuisine, but now read *International Family Talent Night – Come in!* He'd written it himself with the help of his father, and was rather proud of it, pointing it out to every family that entered.

The restaurant was filled with locals and expatriates, eating and drinking merrily as the waiters bustled between tables and kitchen. The lights had been dimmed so that everyone could focus on the spotlighted stage that Mr. Chen had built near the front of the dining room, where a young Chinese girl in a red curly-haired wig was now tap dancing and singing a Shirley Temple song as the audience approvingly looked on.

Aviva stood to the side of the stage in the dark. She couldn't believe she'd managed all of this, and was trying to keep a feeling of pride from swelling up inside her. She hadn't earned pride, not yet. She needed to do more. She had already sat with Mick Ryan and told him the story he wanted to hear: she was an orphan, all alone, a refugee who'd found sanctuary in a foreign land. The story had been published in America and already the rabbi said he was receiving telegrams with promises of donations. And now this fundraiser. But the stones in her chest — one named Samuel, one named Ora — were still there. The stones had taken the place of her heart. She needed to do more.

As the girl on stage started a new verse—*I want to make some noise, with real live airplanes. Some day I'm going to fly*—Rabbi Mesner and Mrs. Borgrov approached her. Aviva tensed. She'd been waiting for what felt like years, but what was really only several day or a week at most, for the rabbi to storm angrily into the restaurant, and chuck her valise at her feet, and throw her journal into her face. *I know who you are*, he would say. *I know what you did.* But here he was, the same smile on his face, the same seemingly never-ending joy in his voice.

"This is absolutely wonderful, Aviva," said the rabbi, embracing her in his usual bear hug as Mrs. Borgrov watched him. In a voice drenched in sarcasm, she asked Aviva if she was going to get up and sign them a song.

But Aviva was used to the woman now. "Only if you'll back me up," she said playfully, to which Borgrov let short breath of air escape from her mouth, the closest thing to a laugh that the woman could manage. The audience clapped as the little girl on stage finished her song, and the rabbi and Mrs. Borgrov turned to the stage to join in on the applause. Aviva surveyed the restaurant and wound her way aimlessly around the tables, desperate for something useful to do. She wondered if there would ever be enough work, enough sweat on her brow, to wipe away her past from her own mind. She'd just decided to go into the kitchen and help the aunties preparing the food, when a hush came over the room and a slow, mournful melody blossomed into the room.

She turned back to the stage and saw a thin, rather pale man under the spotlight, seated at a piano. Everyone had stopped eating, so quietly enraptured by the man's playing that you could almost hear his fingers moving through the air as he smoothly struck each key. The only sound was when a young couple got up from their table, went to the center of the room, unabashedly wrapped their arms around each and slow danced. Aviva seemed to be the only one who noticed them, as everyone else focused intensely on the piano player.

For a moment, the man and woman dancing were Aviva and Erik. Erik kissing her on her nose, Erik's fingers in her hair. She closed her eyes against this unwelcome vision, and kept them closed, afraid that if she opened them again, Erik would be there, his hand outstretched, beckoning her to dance with him. When she opened her eyes again, Erik was gone, and the young couple was still in the center of the room, looking deeply into each other's eyes as if nothing else mattered.

She remembered slow dancing with herself on the

day Paris fell. There was no lush piano melody that day, only the faint sound of gunfire and military orders shouted through the radio in German-accented French. She knew that it would only be a matter of time before the Germans rolled through their street in a tank, and Aviva for some reason had decided that the only response to this was to dance. She picked up Ora, still a newborn then, and swayed slowly from side to side while Samuel sat in his chair, reading a newspaper and rustling it irately. Another German voice sounded through the radio, saying in broken French that all Parisians must stay calm, all Parisians must submit. Samuel shifted nervously in his chair.

"I can't read with such noise," he said.

But Aviva kept dancing, bringing Ora's small face as close to hers as possible. Savoring new motherhood, submitting to the unknown.

"The dancing works," she said. "The dancing keeps her from crying."

She looked over at her husband, and felt a sudden urge to connect with him. This could be their last night together as people who were truly free. Who knew what an occupation would mean, who knew what tomorrow would bring? She laid Ora down in her crib, then went to her husband, kneeling down so that she could look up at him.

"Will you dance with me, Sam?" she asked.

Samuel ignored her, keeping his eyes on the newspaper, whose headline read *PARIS CAPITULATES, NAZIS REIGN*. But Aviva wouldn't move away. She didn't know why, but she felt that if they didn't share some final, intimate moment now, before the Germans arrived, then any potential they might have had to truly love each other would be lost forever.

Finally Samuel glanced down at his wife's hopeful face, then quickly looked away as he stood up. Letting the newspaper fall to the floor, he said, "I will dance when there is music."

A sudden burst of applause pulled Aviva out of her reverie. She watched as the piano player bowed humbly to the audience, and she joined in their applause, clapping with such intensity that the diners nearest her gave her bemused looks. She glanced around the room for the dancing couple, but couldn't see them. She wanted to find them, to wish them well, to tell them to find some safe corner of the earth and hide together from the world.

A new act took the stage and quickly launched into an upbeat cacophony of accordions and drums. Conversation and clinking glasses rose back up from the dining room tables, and Aviva realized that what she needed was air. She needed to breath in something deeply that was not her own memories.

She made her way toward the front door, but just as she got there, Mick Ryan burst in from the street, knocking Little Tao over on his stool. The boy and the stool fell to the floor with a crash, and the music stopped and the revelers all looked toward the door to see what the disturbance could be. What could possibly ruin this fine night, what could there be to fear?

Chen rushed over to help his son to his feet as Mick darted into the restaurant looking wildly around. He was red-faced and breathing heavily, as if he'd run there. He seemed to be in the grip of something, panic or bewilderment or both. As everyone stared at him in gaping silence, he kept opening his mouth but not uttering a sound except for the quick gasping of breath. Finally Aviva put her hands gently on both of his shoulders, and asked him — like a doctor talking to a psychotic patient — what was wrong.

"They've bombed us!" Mick shouted out to the room, as if Aviva's gentle questioning had pressed a release button inside of him. "We're in the war," he said, and then repeated it again to convince himself. "We're in the war!"

All at once, everyone in the restaurant — the

children playing near the stage, the singers playing with their costumes, the families eating their cakes, the waiters serving them—seemed to rise up at once. Some rushed immediately for the door, seeming to know, unlike Aviva, exactly what Mick meant, and what it must mean for them. Others, like Aviva, crowded around Mick and demanded clarity. Who was 'they?' Who was 'we?' What exactly had happened, and when?

Rabbi Mesner came forward and led Mick to a chair, onto which he promptly collapsed.

"The Japanese. On Pearl Harbor," he said, his breath still coming in heaves. "They're saying torpedoes just fell from the sky, no warning."

Aviva imagined the things shaped like deadly, metal sausages she'd seen in government pamphlets, how they must have rained down from above on the people below. The restaurant quickly emptied, until only she and Mick, the rabbi and Mrs. Borgrov, and Chen and Little Tao remained. They didn't speak, each of them lost in their own thoughts, unsure of what to do next, frozen in uncertainty and fear.

Mick thought of Tomoto, how he'd clinked the captain's glass without realizing what he was toasting. Chen thought of Wen Li hiding in his basement, who had probably just received this news from one of his many messengers creeping in through the sewer door, who at this very moment was likely pacing in angry strides beneath the floorboards, knowing that this event meant the Japanese army was growing stronger, more wildly brazen in their attacks, and more dangerous in Shanghai. Rabbi Mesner thought of the young men driving the planes, pressing buttons and releasing death as if it were all a game, as if it—*life*—meant nothing.

Aviva thought of the wars she'd left behind, not the actual one in Europe, but the ones that had been raging inside of her. The war between girlhood and womanhood, between Erik and Samuel, between remembering or forgetting. Was it so wrong of her to feel a sense of relief, that the war in front of her now was not her own, that it was between countries and governments and armies, and that she was of no consequence to any of it? She studied the faces around her. They all, even Borgrov, believed that she was whoever she said she was, and that she was good, and that the people who were bad in this world were the ones in the air with bombs and on the ground with guns. Not her.

They all remained in the dining room for a while longer, the lights still out. They kept a communal silence that each hoped was comforting to the other.

None of them knew what else might be coming, and none of them knew what was already there.

While Aviva and the others were at Mr. Chen's sitting in quiet, darkness and confusion, the German Consulate was brightly lit, a row of cars were parked on the streets outside, and inside the ballroom was filled with music and a gaily swirling crowd of German and Japanese consul officials, high-ranking military, businessmen in tuxedos and their wives in sparkling gowns.

Captain Tomoto stood at the top of a winding staircase with a German general, a short, pudgy man who was fiddling with the cork of a champagne bottle.

They were both drunk: the general from the champagne they'd been consuming all evening as news of the successful attacks came in, and the captain from pride, from pleasure, from the power he felt, even though he was only on the sidelines, he felt as if he himself had driven one of the planes that had torpedoed the American naval base, that stain on the Pacific. It was the most significant move they could have made, as it showed the world that this section of the globe belonged to the Emperor. And it reminded the Germans that Japan was their most formidable ally, a fact that Tomoto sometimes felt was lost on the local German population of Shanghai. During his last stay in this city, the Germans had occasionally demonstrated a certain lack of esteem for their Japanese counterparts, acting as if the Imperial Army were their lesser sidekicks rather than equals. But tonight Tomoto had spent the entire evening with this German general clapping him on the back, pouring him champagne. Asking him if he'd met this girl Frieda, that girl Helga, demanding that the red-cheeked blondes offer Tomoto a dance.

Now the German general was clearing his throat and chiming his glass with a fork he'd giddily grabbed away from a passing waiter. The band quieted down, and everyone in the ballroom turned to look at up at the general and Tomoto.

"To our friends, the Japanese!" the general bellowed out into the ballroom, raising his glass to Tomoto. "May they continue the good fight in triumph and honor. Long live the Emperor!"

The crowd immediately raised their glasses and returned the toast, then the band started up again and the celebration carried on.

Kiyata approached Tomoto and saluted his captain, who gave him a short nod without breaking from his discussion with the general.

"Now is the perfect time for us, *Herr* General, to obtain total control over the International Settlement," Tomoto was saying.

The general nodded happily along. "Yes, yes. And you have our full support, of course." He gestured widely behind him to a row of German soldiers standing silently at attention against a wall. "An additional unit has just arrived from Berlin to assist in providing order during this glorious…this glorious…" The German general drunkenly trailed off, as if he'd momentarily lost his tongue.

It was Kiyata who rescued him. "The glorious *transition?*" said Kiyata, and the German general laughed and clasped him roughly on the back as he called for a waiter to bring the young lieutenant some champagne. Tomoto watched this interaction, annoyed.

Kiyata quickly downed his glass and prepared to dismiss himself from his superior, sensing that his presence was unwelcome. But the German general was now peering at Kiyata as if seeing him for the first time.

"And is the young Lieutenant thoroughly prepared for what's coming next?" he asked.

"Yes, sir," answered Kiyata promptly. "Although—" He broke off for a moment, seeing Captain Tomoto giving him a sharp look. But the champagne had already created a gentle buzz in his brain, and he went on. "Although I suggest showing some restraint," he said. "So as not to antagonize the entire international population in Shanghai against us."

Kiyata watched as Tomoto slowly, deliberately set his glass down on the nearby table, clearly trying to control his anger at the lieutenant's unsolicited advice in front of the German general, who was too drunk to notice the sudden, violent change in Japanese captain's tone.

"Our strategy, *Herr* General, is simple," said Tomoto, addressing the German but staring straight at Kiyata as he forcefully outlined his plan.

They would identify Japan's enemies, who were all of the citizens of the Allied countries in Shanghai. Next, we would investigate their companies, find out who was receiving money, how much money, and from where. Then, they would arrest any suspicious persons who may be spies, and invite them to Bridge House to share their secrets as a guest of Tomoto and the Emperor. And finally, once Tomoto felt sure that he had gathered all of the whispers that he could, they would take over the International Settlement, and crush the resistance movement that had developed underground.

Tomoto glowered at Kiyata, no longer caring if the German general noticed the tension in their ranks. "That is," said Tomoto in a growl, "if it is alright with *the young Lieutenant.*"

With that, Tomoto abruptly walked away, leaving a wary Kiyata behind with the drunkenly confused German general. Kiyata watched as Tomoto menacingly stalked past the row of German soldiers still standing like statues at attention against the wall. Then, Tomoto is gone.

Kiyata knew that he shouldn't have spoken out of turn. But since Tomoto's arrival to Shanghai, he'd had a nagging feeling in the back of his mind that things could soon get out of hand. They already occupied the city, and the International Settlement was the main force for the local economy. What good would it do to damage that?

As the German general drifted off toward a duo of smiling blonde women, Kiyata looked at the line of German soldiers, their uniformed bodies, their polished shoes, their neat caps, and the shining Nazi pins on their lapels. Young men, all of them, though not much younger than Kiyata himself.

Kiyata studied one soldier in particular, who for some reason seemed out of place. Physically he looked no different—tall, yellow hair, light eyes. But the eyes were somewhat vacant, not in a dumb way, but as if the soldier's head was in the clouds, a wispy sort of dreaminess surrounding him that Kiyata unaccustomed to seeing in a German soldier. The young, yellow-haired man was even tapping one foot to the percussionist in the band. If Kiyata had had a soldier with that sort of attitude, he would've been especially harsh with him, given him extra duties and punishments to help keep his feet on the ground, to help bring him back down to earth.

Kiyata shook the thoughts from his head; he had his own soldiers to worry about. He wanted to get out of this ballroom. He wanted to return to Bridge House, where he could dole out and receive orders. Where he could return to his place.

The dreamy German soldier that Kiyata had noticed was still tapping his foot to the beat of the music as the Japanese lieutenant passed by him, close enough to touch.

But the soldier did not notice him, the dreamy look on his face only a cover for a plotting mind. There wasn't much time, and he would have to learn the city quickly, and needed to plan his escape route. He hadn't come to Shanghai to wage war, to help take over some foreign settlement inside of a foreign city being occupied by a foreign invader. Officer Erik Von Strummer — a would-be poet, son of a rich Berliner, who fellow soldiers whispered had been arrested last month on charges of desertion but because of his father had been spared a bullet to the head — was in Shanghai on his own mission, with its own goal.

The goal, the girl, had already slipped through his

fingers once. And he would not allow her to slip away again.

16

The next morning, after the Japanese had attacked Pearl Harbor, and attacked Guam, and attacked Malaya, and Singapore, and Hong Kong, and the Philippines, Japan declared war on America and the United Kingdom, who quickly returned the declarations with ones of their own. China, too, declared war against Japan, and the unofficial battles that had been waged for several years between the two nations were now official. In the newspapers and on the radio they were now called 'The Pacific Theater,' a name that seemed grotesquely comical to Aviva, evoking images of shadow puppetry and kabuki opera instead of the demise and bereavement that war had brought to the nation that Aviva now considered her home.

Panic swept through the International Settlement. Shanghai had belonged to Japan already for years, but this area had always been the city's safest haven—the French Concession, the British and American Quarters, plus the smaller neighborhood pockets of Danes, Italians, British Indians. They'd had their own municipal government, their own police force, their own schools, full autonomy. But now over half the countries in the settlement were at war with the country that ran the city, Japan, the other half at war with or under the dominion of their allies, the Germans.

All morning, rumors whipped through the International Settlement that the Japanese had effectively taken over the area that expatriates believed was theirs. A Japanese soldier had stopped a family walking in the American Quarter and handed them black armbands with the letter A embroidered in white. When the husband explained to the officer that they were British, not American, the Japanese officer had then handed him two black armbands with the letter B, and slid a third one around the small arm of their little daughter.

An Indian accountant was taking a phone call at his desk when two Japanese officers burst inside. One of them yanked the phone from the accountant's hand and slammed it back onto the receiver, while the other officer ripped open every filing cabinet and removed every single piece of paper he could find. As soon as they left, the accountant picked the telephone back up off of its receiver, determined to book the next passage back to Calcutta.

A Dutch journalist had been dragged from his news office, his wrists handcuffed behind his back, and terror on his face.

All of these stories landed in Mr. Chen's Restaurant and Café.

While the kitchen maids prepared breakfast orders upstairs, Aviva sat on the floor of the basement with Tao in her lap, both of them gazing up at Wen Li as he orated passionately. His audience—besides Aviva, Tao, and Mr. Chen—was a dozen of his comrades, a mixture of Chinese and expatriate men, some wearing the black armbands the Japanese had been passing out to identify their nationality: A for American, B for British, N for the Netherlands, X for 'other.' The basement was crowded with shelves of canned goods, tools, and several mounds of rope whose purpose Aviva could not guess. Chen was standing guard at the door that lead up to the kitchen, and Wen Li's comrades sat on wooden crates or on the floor. Wen Li remained standing.

"The Japanese have already demonstrated,"

Wen Li said, "that they are willing to annihilate innocent people with no warning." He paced in the small space, a fierce creature ready to spring from its cage. "Now is the time to strike back before—"

A knock at the door interrupted him. Wen Li's comrades all stood up in unison, as if they were ready for battle. Aviva stood up, too, and tried to hide Little Tao behind her. But he pushed himself up and, copying the men around him, adopted a battle stance that to Aviva looked grossly tragic on the small child's body.

Chen opened the door a crack, through which Mick Ryan poked his head before trying to thrust his whole body inside.

"No journalists allowed," said Chen, holding the door with the weight of his body.

Mick slipped one hand through the door's cracked and waved it as if in surrender.

"I'm not writing any stories, I swear!" he said. "I just want to help." He held up his arm so that everyone in the room could see his A armband. "Look at they're making me wear!" he exclaimed. He thrust his face back through the door, and looked earnestly into the room at Wen Li. "I'm fighting the same fight you are, now."

Chen started to protest again, but Wen Li interjected.

"It's alright," said Wen Li. "Let him in."

Chen eyed Mick suspiciously, but opened the door a little more and let Mick squeeze through as everyone except for Wen Li sat down again.

"Last month," Wen Li continued bitterly, "one of our comrades was killed in that torture chamber run by the Japanese. And what did we do in retaliation?" He looked around at the group gathered before him, a look of dejection coming over his face. "Nothing," he said. "We did nothing." He was silent for a moment, letting his words sink in.

Little Tao moved over to Wen Li and tugged on his hand, and Wen Li finally sat down with a heavy sigh, drawing Tao into his lap as Mick watched them closely.

"We've got to protect our families," Wen Li said while gesturing at Tao, "from any more violence at the kempeitai's hands." He put Tao down and stood up again. "We've got to send a message to the Japanese that their cruelty will not continue. Not in Shanghai." All of his comrades nodded along, everyone except for Aviva, Mick, and Chen.

After a plan was made and the meeting was

finished, Aviva, Chen, and Wen Li spoke in a huddle in one corner of the basement, while in another corner Mick Ryan was playing with Tao, the boy's pet cricket, several tiny cowboy figurines. Chen glanced over at them, then turned back to Wen Li and spoke in a low, warning tone.

"I agree," he said, "that we must make a move against the Kempeitai. But we must be cautious—"

The normally calm Wen Li turned away from Chen in exasperation.

"*Caution*," exclaimed Wen Li. "This Captain Tomoto is becoming more ruthless everyday!" He came back to Chen and put his hands on the older man's soldiers. "I want to confront him. I want to look him in the face. Don't you?"

Aviva watched as a sudden wave of anguish took over Chen's face at the sound of Tomoto's name, and Wen Li removed his hands from the older man's shoulders, embarrassed at having upset his friend. The three of them stood for a moment in silence, and watched as Mick comically swung a piece of rope above his head, tied it into a lasso, handed it to Little Tao.

"Now you're a real American cowboy," said Mick affably, and showed Tao how to swing the lasso over his head and toss it at one of the wooded crates as if it were a heifer on the range.

Finally, Chen turned back to Wen Li. "I'm only saying to be cautious." He looked at Aviva for help.

"Mr. Chen's right," Aviva said. She looked into Wen Li's determined face. "You must stay alive in order to lead."

As if a wave of fatigue had suddenly come over him, Wen Li broke away from them and went to sit down on a crate. For several long moments he sat there, lost in thought. Then he stood back up, and looked directly at Chen.

"One can only go into battle," Wen Li said, "if he is prepared to die to win it." Then he turned to Aviva. "If you could do anything you could to save your own people," he said to her, "I know that you would."

Aviva's face immediately reddened, and she quickly turned away from Wen Li and Chen. She wondered if the shame she felt was visible to them. Did Wen Li know the wound his words were touching inside of her? Of course not. He truly believed that, given the chance, she would act as noble and righteous as he.

She tried to see herself through Wen Li's eyes, through Rabbi Mesner's eyes, through Mr. Chen's: she was the good girl, the fundraiser, the dedicated volunteer, helping take care of Tao.

But it was a lie, all of it.

Unless, somehow, she could make it true.

17

Aviva decided that she would be the girl that Wen Li and Rabbi Mesner saw in her. She had promised to raise funds for the Synagogue of Shanghai. It was hardly a sacrifice, was nothing even remotely close to dangerous work that Wen Li was prepared to do for his people. But still, it was something. Something that *she* could do for hers.

    She left Mr. Chen's and marched determinedly to the International Bank to inquire about the donations that the synagogue had been expecting from America. As she walked along the harbor toward the bank, she felt the tension in the air around her, all of the pedestrians, keeping their heads down and moving quickly along as they passed by several armed Japanese guards menacingly milling around the sidewalks.

When Aviva entered the lobby of the bank, she found a long, rowdy queue of locals and foreigners, a few of them pushing and shoving each other to move forward. She marched over to the back of the line, and planted herself there, and prepared to wait.

~

While Aviva was standing in line at the bank, Rabbi Mesner stood at his office door removing clothing from a battered blue suitcase. He handed the bundle of clothes across the doorway to a waiting family, seven people including the two grandparents and pair or 1-year-old twins. He disliked the way he had begun to count people — *this* was a family of seven, *that* was a family of five. He put every ounce of willpower he had into stopping himself from seeing the refugees in terms of how many mouths he had to feed, how many naked backs he had clothe. He hadn't studied a spiritual passage closely in months. There was no time to be a rabbi when there were rice bags that needed to be rationed, when there were visits to be doled out to any wealthy family, Chinese or foreign, who might be willing to take a family into their home.

Whenever the pressure of the needy refugees seemed like too much for him to bear, he reminded himself of those final days in Germany, how suddenly the realization had hit him that death was marching squarely toward him and his people, and that an exodus was their only chance of survival. His wife had died a few years before the war, and they had never been able to have children. At his age no one pressured him to remarry, nor had he wanted to, and so he had only himself and his rabbinical texts.

But now he was the sole person responsible for the Jewish refugees that continued to stream into Shanghai, now he had a family that ranged into the thousands. He felt a responsibility toward each of them that went beyond mere duty or spiritual love. Was there a word for this feeling? He didn't know. As a child people thought he was brilliant; he seemed to know every word that ever existed in German, in Hebrew, in Yiddish, in Latin. But now words failed him. There was only more work to do, more lives to save, or perhaps only to prolong.

He closed the battered blue suitcase and plucked the identifying card from its side: *Hirsh, Salzburg*. He always tried, and failed, not to wonder too much about the families that never made it there. He didn't want to think of the Hirsh family, who were so sure that they would make it out of Salzburg and reach Shanghai that they had sent their luggage ahead of them. Mr. Hirsh was probably in a work camp on the eastern front; Mrs. Hirsh might be dead from frost. Better to just be grateful for their warm clothes, their sturdy shoes, which now belonged to a family of seven in need.

He picked the next suitcase off the top of the stack, a small, dark red trunk. It was beautiful, he thought, with its blooming flowers painted on the front. He took a simple pleasure in looking at it, and savored that pleasure, knowing how rarely it came to him these days. He plucked the card off the side of the trunk and read it.

Druker, Paris.

He opened the trunk and peered inside. There were a few folded dresses, a pair of woman's shoes, and a small book that had no title on its cover. He removed the shoes and laid them on the floor near the door so that he could locate them easily the next time someone came around needing a pair. He removed the dresses and gave them each a shake, then draped them across the back of a chair. He imagined the small, feminine frame of the woman who must have owned the dresses, and a stir of desire briefly crept up in him, a feeling that felt rather foreign to him after all these years. Why hadn't he remarried? Was he glad that he had no children, after the terrors he had witnessed, and was still witnessing? Perhaps. But if he had remarried, his wife would be here with him now. They would have shouldered these burdens together, and she would've reminded him that he was not only a rabbi, and a caretaker of people seeking refuge, but also a man.

Rabbi Mesner returned to his desk, and picked up the book with no name. As soon as he opened it, something fell from its pages onto his lap, a photo.

He only had to glance at it to know the face of the woman looking back at him. It was a face he had grown to love, the way an old shepherd knows and loves the face of his favorite lamb, no matter how large his flock. Aviva.

But who was that man, and who was that child?

He opened the book, and saw that the words were handwritten.

A knock at the door startled him. It was Mrs. Borgrov. She said that she was only checking in, and how was he doing, and did he need any help?

Rabbi Mesner beckoned her in and told her to close the door.

"Mrs. Borgrov," he said hesitantly. "Can you read French?"

~

Aviva looked into the young, pretty face of a Chinese bank teller, who sat behind a window of bars regarding her with a sympathetic but tired look. Customers in line behind her impatiently pushed forward, smashing her body against the teller station.

"I'm sorry," the bank teller said, "but there are no wire transfers for this account from the United States."

Aviva tried to remain calm, but couldn't keep her voice from growing irate.

"But we were expecting several donations," she exclaimed. "They're coming in from synagogues and people all over America."

The bank teller was already motioning the next customer forward, simultaneously apologizing to Aviva in her polite but distant tone.

Overcome, Aviva suddenly slammed one hand against the teller window bars, then immediately took it away and breathed a heavy, emotional sigh.

She looked into the bank teller's eyes and said simply, and softly, "Please."

The teller studied Aviva for a moment, and then leaned in conspiratorially, speaking in a low voice.

"It's not only you," the teller said. "No one has been able to receive money from American banks."

Aviva considered this for a moment. The rabbi had said this would happen, but they hadn't thought it would be so soon.

Suddenly, a strapping Irish man who had been standing impatiently behind Aviva was forcefully nudging her out of the way. "Come on, honey, next on now!" he said. But then he saw the look of despair on her face, and said more gently, "You should be sending money out, not bringing it in."

Aviva moved out of the line, and took in the surging queue of desperate people that continued to port into the bank lobby, all of them carrying bank notes and passports. She went back out onto the street, and felt something in the air that was beyond tension, that was bordering on chaotic. The streets were filled with people carrying more suitcases than she'd noticed before, all of them seeming to be streaming in one direction, toward the harbor, the same docks where she had arrived to this city with nothing but a shawl around her shoulders and a vow to forget everything that had come before.

She wondered how she would face Rabbi Mesner. She felt that she had let him down somehow, that she had failed him and the Synagogue of Shanghai. She would have to go to him tomorrow and explain what the bank had said, that there would be no money, that they were totally on their own now. She didn't think she could bear it, bringing him such disappointing news. But it was her duty; this was her responsibility. Already she was imagining the dismay on his face, but still, he wouldn't blame her, she knew. He would probably open his arms wide and pull her into a hug, and tell her that he knew she had tried her best, and that it was all right. That everything would be all right.

~

Mrs. Borgrov took the journal from Rabbi Mesner. "From the beginning?" she asked.

He shook his head, no, choose any page, any entry.

She opened the book to a random page and squinted at the writing, reading several lines to herself and translating it in her head before speaking.

"Erik doesn't really believe in the Nazi cause, of course," Mrs. Borgrov read aloud. "He joined the army to leave Germany, not fight for it. He only cares about poetry, and music, and art, and love." She stopped to cough. "He only cares about loving me." She stopped and looked to the rabbi to see if she should continue, and he nodded, so she did.

Rabbi Mesner listened intently as she read. It seemed to have been written that year, definitely during the summer, in what exact location, he didn't know. The journal entry was about a picnic that the owner of the journal—Aviva?—had taken with this man, this Erik, this Nazi. The prose was so detailed that he could clearly see the scene unfolding before him as Borgrov spoke.

Aviva and Erik on a lushly green open field, the sun shining brightly down on them as they frolicked across the grass. Then they lay together cuddled up on a picnic blanket, stomachs full from their feast. Then Erik said to her, "I've got one last surprise for you, but you've got to close your eyes." So Aviva closed her eyes. She asked what the surprise was, but he wouldn't tell her, and she felt like a child, and she liked that feeling. Then she heard the crinkle of something being unwrapped, and she whispered, "I can hear it."

Then suddenly there was silence, and Rabbi Mesner opened his eyes—he hadn't realized his eyes were closed—and saw that Mrs. Borgrov had stopped reading and was staring at him.

"Go on!" the rabbi barked at her, and then immediately regretted it. But he said it again, in a softer, sadder voice. "Go on."

Aviva heard the snap of something being broken in half, and then something smooth that smelled of coco was at her lips, then teasingly taken away. She started to remove her hands from her eyes, but Erik said sternly, "No. Keep them closed." And she obeyed him. He brought the chocolate back to her lips, and when she tried to lick it he pulled it away again, causing her to lean forward and lick at the air. Even with her eyes closed, she could feel the intensity of his gaze on her, always on her. Now he was whispering, "You have to come find me, Aviva." She stuck out her tongue again, and curled it repeatedly into the air until he pushed the chocolate gently back to her lips, and sweetness filled her mouth. He drew the chocolate away again, leaned in close to her face and whispered, "I'm right here in front of you. I'm right here."

Rabbi Mesner raised a hand, signaling to Mrs. Borgrov to stop.

He looked again at the photo, then turned it over, and saw that something was written on the back: *Samuel, Aviva, & Ora Druker, 1941.*

"Enough," he said, though Borgrov had already fallen silent. "I've heard enough."

18

At Mr. Chen's Restaurant and Café, Little Tao peaked through the kitchen doors into the dining room, and watched as a table of three Japanese officers chatted and drank tea, waiting for their meals.

Tao was alone in the kitchen. Aviva was gone, and the remaining kitchen maids were doing double duty in the dining room, as their staff had quickly thinned due to several waiters deciding that now was the time to leave Shanghai. The diners, too, had thinned; there was an exodus occurring, or about to occur, in Shanghai.

But Little Tao was not thinking of his. He dragged a chair over to a cupboard, climbed on top of the chair, and rummaged through the various cans, spices, and condiments until he found what he was looking for: a jar identical to the one he'd found in the trash bin the month before, the same drawing of a black rat on one side of the jar, the skull and bones on the other side.

Tao dragged the chair from the cupboard over to the stove, climbed on top of the chair, and looked down into the opaque surface of a boiling pot of soup. He tried to open the lid of the rat poison jar, but it was screwed on too tightly for his small, soft fingers. But he didn't give up, and was still trying to unscrew the jar when his father walked in.

Chen ran over to his son and lifted him off the chair. The jar slipped from Tao's hand and fell to the floor, smashing into pieces as it hit.

Chen set Little Tao down on the ground, and began to shake him roughly by the shoulders.

"What do you think you're doing?" Chen said. But Tao looked away from him, held captive by his father's grip but still refusing to speak, knowing that no one could force him. "You think you're a killer? You think that's brave?" Chen was screaming now. "Answer me!"

Tao only stared up at his father, his face contorted in anger. Chen had never seen his son look at him like that. It was enough to bring him tears. He grabbed Tao and hugged him tightly, and after a beat, Tao hugged him back.

"You think I can't fight the Japanese man that took your mother?" Chen asked tearfully into the top of his son's head. He felt his son shake his head, No.

"So you think you have to fight him for me?" Chen felt his son nod his head, Yes.

Tao pulled himself from his father's embrace. He went to one of the kitchen closets and pulled it out a broom, and slowly began sweeping up the broken jar while his father watched him. The boy's shoulders heaved, and Chen realized his son silently sobbing.

"Let me do it," said Chen, taking the broom away from his son. "I haven't seen that cricket lately, is he still alive?"

Tao, of course, did not answer him. Every day he renegotiated a deal with himself over when he would start to speak again. Before, the deal had been to start speaking whenever his mother came back home. Then, it was whenever the Japanese left Shanghai. Then, it was when his father made good on his promise to tell him why and how his mother had died. But now he felt that none of his deals would work, and that he would have to live for the rest of his life in silence. He didn't mind it, not really. He told himself that he didn't need to speak. He could cook, he could now tie a lasso and toss it with some success onto an unmoving target, he could write. He didn't need to make his words into sounds. There was enough noise in the world already. His silence was good. Silence made sense. Only sometimes, he let himself wonder: what would he have sounded like if he had ever learned to sing?

Later on in the day, as evening approached, Chen stood at the counter halfheartedly chopping fresh figs. The kitchen was empty again, and the hum of restaurant noise could be faintly heard in the dining room. Chen couldn't stop glancing over at the spot near the stove where he'd found Tao earlier. He'd put a new pot of soup on to boil, but the sense of unease had still not left him. Look at what his own inaction had driven his son to consider. It was his own fault.

He stopped chopping and sat down with a heavy, tired sigh, and put his face into his hands. When he looked back up, Su was standing at the stove. She was stirring the pot, and looked over at him with a mild smile and shook her head knowingly.

"Our boy," said Su. "He's really something, isn't he?"

This time, Chen did not feel alarmed or scared. It was almost as if he'd expected to see her. He knew by now that it was just his mind, grieving, playing tricks on him. Su continued stirring as she spoke.

"You have to help him understand," she said.

A sudden wellspring of anger opened up inside of him. "Understand what?" he hissed at her. He'd never spoken to her that way when she was alive. "Why you left us? Even I don't understand that."

Su put down the spoon and came over to Chen. She stood directly in front of him and smiled kindly down on him, and suddenly Chen was less sure that she wasn't real. He looked up at her, his eyes pleading.

"Tell me why," he said. "Did he take you? Or did you want to go…"

Su softly shushes him, putting a finger to his lips.

"You'll find out," she said. "All you have to do is ask him."

Him. Tomoto.

"Besides," she went on, "I'm here now."

Su picked up a piece of fig from the table, then brought it to Chen's lips.

"I'm right here in front of you," she said.

Chen ate the fig from Su's fingers, then stood, and wrapped his arms around her. They stood there for several long moments, and Chen thought of the life they'd had together, the life that Tomoto had stolen from him.

Little Tao was sitting on the steps that led up to the family apartment. He had been sitting there for several minutes, watching his father chopping fruit, watching his father talk to someone. Now, his father was reaching out his arms, and wrapping them around an empty space, as if to hold someone.

That night, Chen came down into the basement as Wen Li and his comrades were preparing to leave. They had knives, a few pistols, and several glass bottles filled with petrol and stuffed with a rag. A few them had ripped the black embroidered armbands from their sleeves.

"I'm coming with you," said Chen.

Wen Li didn't hide his surprise. "Good," he said. "I'll need your help."

He handed Chen a long dagger, and Chen studied his reflection in the steel.

Aviva bounded downstairs into the basement. She'd stayed around the docks for the rest of the afternoon into the evening, watching as ship after ship took what seemed like hundreds of passengers away. One was headed to Australia, another was going to South Africa, with several stops in between. There was an exodus occurring, and she didn't understand why.

"Mr. Chen—"

She stopped herself at the sight of his dagger, and he quickly hid it away.

"Aviva," he said. "Will you watch over Tao until I return?"

Aviva looked around at the men in the room. They had their weapons, they had their plans. "Of course I will," she said. "But at the harbor, it seems—"

"We have to leave now," Wen Li said to Chen, cutting Aviva off.

Wen Li and his comrades filed out one-by-one through the door that led into the sewers. Chen started to follow them, then stopped and looked back to Aviva.

"Thank you," he told her.

Aviva bit back her warnings, knowing it was futile to try and stop them, that her observations were irrelevant to Chen, to Wen Li.

So Aviva only nodded. "I'll keep him safe," she said. "I promise."

19

Chen, Wen Li, and the other men sneak stealthily crept through the dark, empty streets. The Japanese had instituted a curfew throughout the International Settlement, and they hid in alleyways and behind trash bins and the occasional car whenever they heard the footsteps of a Japanese soldier out on patrol. But for long stretches the streets were theirs, and they fanned out across the road, a row of men with their weapons drawn, reclaiming their city.

But when they arrived at Bridge House, their

bravado left them. The Kempeitai were a secret police force, and their headquarters was supposed to be a secret—though all of Shanghai knew where it was—and so from the outside the building appeared unguarded. No armed soldiers standing at attention, no locked gate, none of the protection of the consulate or the Imperial Army's official military barracks. It was this stark nakedness, the simplicity of Bridge House, that suddenly made it seem like a trap. A few of the men started arguing in fierce whispers. Didn't people go in there that were never heard from again? Hadn't their own comrade disappeared into this place? They should think this through.

Chen remained silent and stood apart from the others, studying the building that he knew held Tomoto. He had walked all this way, and he was going into Bridge House whether the others were coming or not. It was answers he sought, not vengeance. Not yet.

Wen Li was trying to silence the men when suddenly one of them broke away from the group, a Russian with long hair and a wild look in his eyes who had been arguing that they move forward with the plan. He crouched down low as he moved quickly and quietly toward the building. Chen soon followed, then Wen Li, then the others, and like that it was decided.

They made there way toward the only window on the bottom floor that was lit. Chen, Wen Li, and the wild-eyed Russian peeked over the window ledge and looked inside. It was an office, heavily decorated in the Japanese style, the lights on but the desk vacant.

"Tomoto's office?" Wen Li mused in a whisper.

Before Chen could answer him, the Russian broke the glass window and lit the petrol soaked rag bottle on fire.

"Wait!" hissed Wen Li. But the Russian was already tossing the burning bottle into the room. Immediately, it burst into flames.

The men, led by the Russian, lifted themselves over the window ledge and into the building as Chen and Wen Li watched with frustration. Wen Li had wanted an orderly attack, a mission with clear goals of finding whatever evidence they could regarding the Japanese plans for Shanghai and the rest of China, and to send a message to Tomoto that the city would not simply kneel to him without a fight. But things were already out of control, and Chen and Wen Li hoisted themselves through the window into the office, finding flames already creeping up the walls.

The men were filing out of the office into the hallway, but Wen Li immediately went to the desk and began to pull out every document he could find. It was information that he sought. Chen went to the doorway and watched the men filing down the hallway, their weapons raised. In the other direction was a staircase. He looked back into the office at Wen Li, at the fire that for now seems contained in one corner of the room.

"Go," said Wen Li. "I'll be fine."

For a moment Chen hesitated, watching Wen Li pouring over the documents as the fire crept up a wall on the far side of the room. "Be careful," Chen told him. Then he left him there, and crept stealthily up the stairs.

Chen peaked into the quiet, empty hallway from the stairs. It looked like a hotel, with a long strip of ornate carpet running down the center of the hardwood floors and a black phone atop a single, gilded nightstand. He understood why the other men thought it was a trap. Where were the soldiers, where was anyone?

He padded silently down the hallway, his dagger out. He stopped at every door, opened it if it was closed, looked inside and then moved on to the next one. Empty, all of them. Finally, at the end of the hallway Chen came to one door slightly ajar, a light on inside.

On the other side of the door, Captain Tomoto sat in a bathtub filled to the brim with hot water, enjoying the steam that wafted up to his face. His eyes were closed, his head laid back, completely relaxed. He wasn't celebrating the success of phase one of the International Settlement takeover. And his mind wasn't plotting out the next phase, because that planning was already done; they had only to execute it. His mind was in Tokyo. He was thinking of the girl waiting for him there. He'd left her tied to a beam in his cellar, and had instructed his servants to keep her well-fed and clean until his return. He liked his girls clean, so that he knew that every mark on them had come from him.

A creak in the floorboards outside the bathroom door broke him out of his thoughts. .

"Who's there?" he called out.

Silence.

Tomoto looked his pistol in its holster, hanging on a chair on the other side of the bathroom. He heard another light movement on the other side of the door, and suddenly he felt totally vulnerable and genuinely afraid. When was the last time he'd felt this way?

"Kiyata?" he called out, his voice wavering. "Is that you?"

Inch by inch, Tomoto started to lift himself from the bathtub, never taking his eyes from the door.

In the hallway, Chen put one hand on the doorknob and raises his dagger, ready to attack.

Suddenly, gunfire rang out downstairs. Chen ran back to the stairway and looked over the railing to see several armed Japanese soldiers moving quickly through the hallway downstairs.

Before he could figure out what was happening, what he should do, a gunshot exploded from behind him, it's bullet blowing a hole into the wallpaper near his head.

Without looking back, Chen ran in the opposite direction of the gunfire, down the hallway toward an open window at the other end. He hopped over the ledge, but hesitated as he looked out into the black night, unable to see how far he was from the ground.

From behind him another gunshot exploded, and the window above him shattered as the bullet hit. He jumped.

Tomoto strode fiercely down the hall toward the shattered window, a towel wrapped around his waist, his pistol raised.

Outside, Chen landed in the grass with a hard thud, but quickly got up and started running. The sound of a low, painful moan stopped him, and he turned back to see two bodies lying nearby. One body was moving, the other was still.

Tomoto leaned out of the window. He couldn't

see anything through the thick blackness of the night. But still he aimed his pistol in the direction that his would-be attacker would've fallen, and pulled the trigger. But there was only the soft click of the empty chamber. He tried the trigger a few more times, then threw the pistol at the wall in frustration. He started back toward his room to get dressed, but then voice sounded outside.

"Wen Li!"

Tomoto stopped dead in his tracks. He went back to the window, peered into the dark, and listened.

Outside, Chen looked down at his strong, young friend, who was writhing in pain on the ground. "Wen Li!" Chen cried out again.

He didn't know what to do. Blood was seeping through the front of Wen Li's shirt. He glanced at the other body, the still one. It was the Russian, a single bullet wound visible on the man's forehead. Where were the others?

Chen knew he had to act. He started dragging Wen Li away from the Russian's dead body, back toward Bridge House. Wen Li tried to wrench himself away.

"What are you doing?" Wen Li cried. "Get out of here, just leave me!"

Chen shushed him. "Be quiet," he whispered. "Save your breath for yourself." He kept dragging Wen Li until they were behind Bridge House.

On the front side of the building, a cadre of Kempeitai officers came spilling outside and began searching the streets. Chen knew when one of their comrades had been found, because a flurry of gunfire filled the air. They'd found three of the men so far.

Chen pressed his hand onto Wen Li's stomach, trying to stop the bleeding.

"It's alright, it's alright," he whispered into Wen Li's ear. "I think the bullet went through."

Wen Li said nothing, only grimaced in pain.

Chen felt a wave of guilt as the sound of a man screaming and gunfire filled the air. Four men found. "I should never have left you," he said to Wen Li.

Wen Li made a soft gurgling sound, and Chen realized that he was trying to speak.

"What?" said Chen. "What is it?" He leaned in close and watched his friend's mouth, trying to read the words on his lips.

"They'll find us here," Wen Li finally got out with enormous effort, and then spat a mouthful of blood into the grass.

Chen shushed him again. He rocked the young man they would rock Tao when the boy couldn't sleep.

"Don't worry," he said soothingly, and hoped that he was telling him the truth. "They won't look where they live."

20

The next morning, a fat hand shook Aviva from out of her sleep. She opened her eyes to find herself in the dining room, morning light pouring in through the windows, and Auntie One staring sourly down at her.

"Why don't you sleep in your own bed, girl?" said One.

Aviva started to explain that she and Little Tao had stayed up waiting for Mr. Chen to come home. But Auntie One shushed her, and pointed to a still sleeping Tao sprawled across two chairs. Aviva started to stand up, but found Tao's roped wrapped loosely around her body, and she vaguely remembered his pet cricket crawling around in her hands as Tao played with his lasso, tossing it at her shoulders over and over again until it had finally landed once, then twice. Aviva unwrapped the lasso from around her and stood. She had fulfilled one duty for Mr. Chen, and now she need to fulfill her duty to Rabbi Mesner.

"I have to go out," she said.

Auntie One was already picking up Little Tao. She started toward the kitchen with the boy still asleep in her arms, and said over soldier to Aviva, "So go."

Aviva was at the door when she heard the kitchen maid's voice again.

"But be careful," said One. "There's madness at the harbor. Don't go that way."

Aviva nodded and thanked her, and started out on the long walk. The streets were emptier than the day before, quieter. Maybe Auntie One was wrong, maybe the madness had already subsided. The sun was bright for December, and Aviva took her time walking to the synagogue, thinking of Mr. Chen and Wen Li and whether they'd been able to get what they needed from that place, Bridge House, and from that man, Tomoto. She thought of her Cousin Ruby, the way she came home after a long day's work, tired, but pride showing through the tiredness. She wondered if Cousin Ruby would be proud of her of her if she could see her here in Shanghai, if she could erase what had happened to Samuel and Ora and her reasons for coming to Shanghai, and only keep everything good that she had done since she arrived.

~

As Aviva made her way toward the Synagogue of Shanghai, a young Chinese newsboy was pacing in front of a brown brick building with a small sign over the door that read *American Morning Post*. He struggled with a large stack of newspapers in one hand, and with the other waved a single newspaper in the air.

"Paper here!" he yelled with enthusiasm. "Get your American Morning *pa*-per here!"

But the street was empty of customers. It was so quiet, in fact, that the boy could hear the loud, hesitant clack of a single typewriter coming from inside.

Inside the newsroom, Mick Ryan spun around in his chair. When he got dizzy, he rached out and grabbed his desk to stop the spinning, and come face-to-typewriter with his unfinished article, which he had titled "Underground Resistance Rises in Shanghai." It had a nice ring to it, he'd thought, and his editor agreed. But now he found he was having trouble getting anything significant onto the page.

The newspaper office was small, and empty except for Mick and his boss, the editor, both of them wearing black 'A' armbands over their sleeves. The other desks were vacant, and Mick wished for a distraction, for a reason to procrastinate writing the article that he'd promised was going to put the paper on the map. The editor was reviewing his own article, pointedly ignoring the young journalist except to tell him to get back to work.

"Get it done, Mick," the editor droned without looking up from his work, as if he had some kind of internal clock telling him when Mick needed a push in the right direction.

"Hey, you wanna write it?" Mick shot back, but quickly returned to typing.

In front of the building, the newsboy was still pacing and yelling for someone, anyone, to come and buy a paper from him. Just as he decided that he would ask the editor permission to move to another street, a car came speeding down the street and stopped directly in front of him. There was a rising sun emblem painted on its hood, Japanese. Still, a car was a car, and the boy admired it closely as Captain Tomoto, Lieutenant Kiyata, and two soldiers emerged from the dark seats inside.

It seemed as if the Japanese men didn't see the newsboy standing in front of them, or else that his existence was so trivial to them that they could even bother to stop when Tomoto and the other brushed past the boy, causing him to lose his already precarious balance and fall to the ground, sending the newspapers flying into the air like a sudden takeoff of white, spotted birds.

Tomoto burst inside the newsroom, Kiyata and the soldiers following closely behind, their rifles already raised.

Mick and the editor both jumped up from their desks. The editor immediately raised his hands in surrender, and Mick followed suit, but then the editor realized that he looked undignified and put his hands back down, which Mick also copied, so that they looked like a bad comedic duo whose timing was off.

Tomoto and Kiyata headed straight for Mick, and Kiyata trained is rifle on the journalist while the other soldiers held the editor up against the wall.

The editor caught Mick's eye, and gave him a look that said *Please, just don't say anything stupid*. Mick glanced from his boss, to Tomoto, to Kiyata, and then back to Tomoto.

"Came to give us a scoop?" Mick asked brightly.

The editor rolled his eyes and released a loud, exasperated sigh, feeling rather confident that both of them were going to die.

Tomoto pushed Mick violently back down into his chair.

"You're very lucky today," Tomoto began, "because I really don't have much time to spend on you."

Now the editor looked intrigued, the consummate journalist.

"Oh yeah?" said the editor. "And why's that?" But his words were cut short by a sharp jab to his chest by the soldier's rifle.

"I'm looking for a man named Wen Li," Tomoto continued. "He tried to visit me last night, but I was unable to properly greet him." He casually picked up an old issue from Mick's desk and quickly scanned the headline: *Aviva & The Synagogue of Shanghai*. He studied the photo of the girl underneath the headline, who was beautiful but looked frightened of the camera. He briefly imagined the girl in the photo tied up in his cellar, but he batted the image away.

He was having trouble keeping his focus; too much was happening at once. He needed to find Wen Li now, not only because he leading the resistance, but because he had made Tomoto feel a fear so sharp, brief though it was, that he had momentarily lost all confidence in himself. And the only way to get it back was to wrap his fingers around Wen Li's throat. He tossed the newspaper to the floor and looked back at Mick. "I've heard that you may know where I can find this man."

Mick glanced at the unfinished article still sitting in his typewriter, its headline about the Resistance movement in Shanghai seeming to blare from the page. Tomoto was now circling Mick's desk, and Mick spun his chair around slowly, matching Tomoto's pace. Kiyata watched as Mick leaned back over desk, as if he was trying to keep the typewriter hidden from view.

"Tell me where he is," said the captain, glowering.

"Look," Mick said, "I honestly have no idea—"

Before he could finish, Tomoto lunged for Mick's throat. He started to choke him, almost lifting him up out of his chair by the neck.

Kiyata ripped the pages from the typewriter, quickly skimmed its headline, and rushed around to the other side of the desk where Tomoto now had Mick on the floor.

He called the captain's name, then tried thrusting the unfinished article into his face for him to see. Tomoto violently pushed Kiyata away, and the lieutenant stumbled backward in shock. One of the soldiers caught him, and straightened him up.

Finally, Tomoto released Mick, who crawled around on the floor gasping for breath.

Kiyata, too, felt that he could barely breath. The captain had pushed him, in front of his own subordinates. In front of Americans.

He tensed as Tomoto came over to him and snatched the paper from his hands. As Tomoto studied it, Kiyata openly glared at him.

But Tomoto didn't notice, his attention on Mick. He waved the article in front of the journalist's face. "Do you still say you don't know Wen Li?"

Without waiting for an answer from Mick, Tomoto ordered Kiyata to arrest him.

Kiyata didn't move. He was afraid that if he lifted a finger, that it would be his own hands tightening around Tomoto's throat. The soldier who had caught Kiyata before he fell stepped forward, pulled Mick up off the floor, and handcuffed him, as if Tomoto had given him the order.

Tomoto was already heading for the door. The soldiers—one carrying their rifles, the other guiding Mick by out his handcuffed wrists—followed Tomoto, too embarrassed for Kiyata to look at him.

Kiyata looked at the editor, who had plopped down on the floor in a daze as soon as the rifles were no longer pointed at his chest. Kiyata started to leave, but stopped as the editor spoke.

"What should I do?" the editor asked him.

Kiyata looked at man sitting pitifully on the floor like a child. He wasn't sure if he meant what to do about Mick, or what to do about his newspaper, or what to do to save his own life in case Tomoto decided to come back for him.

"You should leave Shanghai," Kiyata said, and started again toward the door. "You should have already left."

21

Aviva was only a few blocks away from the synagogue when she turned a corner, and saw Mick Ryan being dragged out of a building at the far end of the street. She stopped dead in her tracks with a gasp, and placed over a hand over her mouth to stop herself from crying out.

She watched as a young Japanese soldier tried to push Mick into a car, but Mick dropped to his knees in weak protest, refusing to get in. An older man in a captain's uniform — he looked familiar to her, where had she seen him before? — kicked the Mick in the stomach, and he fell forward onto the ground.

Even with such a distance between them Aviva and Mick locked eyes, his face pushed against the gravel road, hers gone white. The soldier finally managed to drag Mick into the car, and as the car revved to life and turned around, Aviva realized that it was heading straight toward her.

Aviva quickly moved back around the corner from which she'd come, trying hard not to seem panicked and draw attention to herself. Once around the corner, she pressed herself up against the brick wall of a building, and watched as the car sped past her. She started to breath again.

She didn't know what to do now. She wondered who she should tell first, Mr. Chen or Rabbi Mesner? She was closer to the synagogue, and didn't know if Mr. Chen had even returned home yet, so she decided to press onward. The rabbi what know what to do.

She hurried blindly back around the corner, her mind spinning in confusion, but was immediately halted when she ran into the tall body of a uniformed man. She kept her head down and tried to pass by him, but the man in uniform grabbed her by the arm.

As soon as he touched her, she knew. Her eyes still on the ground, she saw his shiny leather shoes, tightly laced in the German standard. Her eyes traveled slowly up his body, the trim waist, the barrel chest, a Nazi pin on the lapel of his collar. The hard jaw that immediately softened as he smiled down at her.

Aviva looked up at Erik in shock. Slow and unsteady, she began to back away from him into the street.

"No." She thought it was only to herself, but heard her own voice and realized she was talking out loud. She said it again, the only word that could find itself from her brain to her lips. "No."

He seemed, like her, to not be able to say more than one word at a time. "Aviva," said Erik, moving toward her just as slowly as she was moving away. "Aviva."

At the sound of her name slipping from Erik's mouth with an intimacy that sickened her, Aviva began to run. She could hear his footsteps pursuing her, and in a queer moment of lucidity — the kind of clarity of thought that pervades one's mind in states of deep fear — she realized that she was running toward the synagogue, and that he would follow her there. When she got to the street that would have taken her to the synagogue if she'd turned left, she turned right.

As soon as she did, she found herself facing a large lumbering tank at the far end of the street, it's cannon pointed straight up into the air, a Japanese flag waving from the top. Where was she? What was happening?

She'd stopped running only for a second, but it was enough time for Erik to catch up to her and grab her from behind. He seemed strangely calm to her, as if he knew exactly what was happening, and why.

He tried to pull her down the street away from the tank, and she tried to rip herself away, then shrieked at him to let go. Didn't anyone hear her? The street seemed deserted except for the tank, but the air was filled with expectation, as if everyone were in hiding waiting for some secret signal, a signal that was at least secret to her.

"You have to come with me," he said steadily in the face of her screams. "They're getting ready to—"

But she'd managed to free herself from his grasp. She had to choose whether to try to run around him, or to run toward the tank. She chose the tank.

She'd only taken a few steps when the tank cannon fired a single blast into the sky, and a cadre of Japanese soldiers came spilling out from behind it, marching in unhurried formation toward Aviva and Erik, bayonets drawn.

Erik again grabbed her, and this time Aviva was too afraid and confused about what was unfolding before her to resist. But she whipped around furiously when he said her name again.

"What?" she roared into his face.

Erik was momentarily stunned by the intensity of her fury. He realized that he hadn't thought of how she would receive him, he just wanted to get to her. And he had. But there was a willfulness emanating from her that he hadn't seen in her before. The cadre of marching soldiers was still approaching, though he knew from his superiors that the Japanese mission did not included shooting expatriates at random on the street. This was the final phase of their takeover of the International Settlement, an exercise in instilling fear and displaying power, to show the international population that now was the time to leave Shanghai, or submit. After he'd slipped away from his own unit who were manning the chaos at the harbor, he'd decided to stay in his uniform in case he ran into any belligerent Japanese soldiers or Kempeitai officers looking for spies. Aviva was still staring at him, a look of fury and questioning on her face.

"Run," he said.

The tank cannon fired another blast. But this time it was not a warning shot into the gray, still sky, but into a building that instantly shattered into a pile of brick and rubble near Erik and Aviva. They ran.

They rounded a corner, only to find another

cadre of soldiers marching up the street.

Just ahead of Aviva and Erik stood a school with a British flying over the doorway, and they quickly ducked inside.

They tried to walk calmly through the hallway, passing classrooms filled with British and a few Chinese students listening to teachers lecturing at the front in crisp, English accents.

The same door through which they had entered opened behind them, and the soldiers they'd seen outside came stampeding in.

"They're coming for us," Aviva whispered to Erik in a panic.

"They're not," he replied, and pulled Aviva into a broom closet, closing the door behind them and leaning the weight of his body against it.

Aviva pulled immediately pulled away from him and pressed herself into the wall, putting as much distance between them as possible. Her mind was a jumble of pieces that didn't fit.

"What's happening?" she demanded, and Erik quickly told her as much as he knew. The Japanese would not allow the citizens of the countries they were at war against to live peacefully here. There would be no more International Settlement; the ninety-year-old agreement granting lands to foreign countries was now null and void. Unless, of course, the country was Japan.

Her mind spun as she considered this. She should've known, they all should've known. They'd thought the inroads into the Settlement would stop at handing out armbands and jailing Allied citizens at random, but no. The Imperial Army wanted total control over every part of Shanghai, because without it, how could the entire country of China be called theirs? Aviva had seen for herself the masses of people boarding ships at the harbor. Europe unsafe, Asia unsafe. They would keep boarding ships until there was nowhere left to go.

Aviva felt calmer now, and regarded Erik with a coolness that felt foreign to her, but right.

"What are you doing here?" she said.

He started to move toward her, put she raised a hand to stop him.

"I got myself into a regiment being sent here," he explained, the same pride in his plotting and planning that she'd seen in him before. "But I snuck away, Aviva. To find you!" He said this last part with such a childish glee that she had to look away.

They quieted as the sound of footsteps marched past their hiding place. Once they were gone, Erik ducked his head out into the school hallway, saw that was clear, and motioned for Aviva to follow him. He started down the hall, but Aviva quickly and quietly moved in the opposite direction, and was already several paces away before he realized that she was not with him. She heard the squeak of his shoes against the floor as he turned back to pursue, but when she glanced back she saw a small group of soldiers entering the hallway from the stairwell, not paying any attention to Aviva on one side of them or to Erik on the other, but their bodies forming a wall between them as they congregated and conferred in low voices. She continued down the hall, relief washing over her as she moved further and further away from Erik. She had to get out of here, before he got to her again.

Aviva passed by the same classrooms as before, but now they each had a single Japanese soldier standing at the front of the room with the British teacher, and the teachers were reading haltingly from a document while the soldier menacingly looked on. Aviva only caught snippets: *You are now under the direction of the Emperor. All children under thirteen are to study Japanese.* The students' eyes were wide with fear and confusion, and they looked how Aviva felt.

At the exit door Aviva burst back out onto the street and looked wildly around, trying to get her bearings, her sense of direction. A truck guarded by a few armed soldiers stood at the end of the street in the direction she thought she should be going. She looked up and saw that the British flag had been replaced by a Japanese one, white and red and waving in the wind.

Suddenly Erik was in front of her again. He moved quicker than she could, and was on a single-minded mission to pursue her, and she realized that continuing to run from him was futile. If she did, she'd be running for the rest of her life. She turned on him, no longer angry or afraid, only exhausted.

"You have to leave, Erik," she said, all the fury gone from her voice. "You just have to go back. Go home, Erik!"

He shook his head. Didn't she understand all that he'd risked for her? He'd done it once in Paris, and after she deserted him he'd gotten caught as he'd tried to slip back into his barracks, his neck only saved by the grace of his last name and his father's money. Now he'd done it again, and there was no going back. Not this time.

"I'm not leaving without you," he said. And his voice was filled with such certainty, such conviction, that she knew that it was true. He would never leave her alone. She didn't want to admit it, but part of her was moved by his devotion, by the risks he kept taking to be with her.

But, Samuel. But, Ora.

Everything about her and Erik was wrong, and could never be made right. She was a deer with one leg clenched by the teeth of a steel trap, the rest of her body technically free but still unable to leap forward, only flailing in place.

A round of gunfire erupted near the armed truck, and Aviva and Erik looked over to see a line of men being led from a building at gunpoint.

"We should find a place to hide," Erik said. "At least until this siege is over."

Erik took Aviva's hand and led her down the street, away from the gunfire and armed truck. He was no longer pulling her, because she was no longer resisting.

Down a residential alley they tried a few doors, and finally found one open, a small apartment that looked recently abandoned. Two bowls of porridge still sat on the table, and a chair had fallen backward onto the floor. Erik did a quick check of the home to make sure no one was hiding out, then closed all the windows, drew the single curtain. Aviva watched him and leaned against the wall, then sank to the floor and put her head in her hands.

Erik didn't know what to do. She seemed unreachable. He went to the wall opposite her and sat down on the floor so that they faced each other, so that they seemed like equals, in this together. For a while they listened to the distant sounds of gunfire and cannon blasts, which eventually quieted down. Finally, hesitantly, he broke the silence.

"At the harbor, there's a ship," Erik said. "The last one to America."

When she didn't respond, he went on. "I've booked us passage," he said. "We can—"

Abruptly Aviva looked up and stared at him. She didn't say anything, but the look on her face was enough to halt his speech. Finally, she spoke.

"How many people have you killed?" she asked quietly.

Erik looked astonished by the question, and didn't answer her.

"Did you know their names?" she continued.

He still said nothing, only stared at her, and she held his stare until he looked away.

"Well," she said, "I have killed two people. Their names were Samuel, and Ora."

Erik remained silent, refusing to meet her gaze. But she didn't stop.

"Did you hear what I said?" she asked. She

stood up and slowly started toward him, but he stayed seated on the floor.

"I said that their names were Samuel and Ora." Now she was standing over him, and he finally looked up at her.

"Say their names," she said.

Erik looked bewildered. "Aviva, I don't—"

"No!" she cut him off, and repeated her command. "Say their names."

He could only hold her angry gaze for a moment before looking away again. She watched as something resembling shame crept over his face. That was a start, but it wasn't enough.

Aviva began to beat her fists against the top of his head, on his back, his arms. She pummeled him. She knew she wasn't really hurting him, and wished that she was stronger.

"Say their names, goddamn you." She was screaming now. "Say their names!"

Erik stood and grabbed her by her wrists. He pinned her arms to her sides and gripped her tighter every time she struggled against him, until she stopped struggling. Their faces were practically touching, so close that she could feel his breath against her lashes as he finally spoke.

"Their names," he said slowly, looking deeply into her eyes, "were Samuel, and Ora."

Now it was Aviva who could not hold his gaze. But he went on.

"And your name is Aviva," said Erik. "And you're the woman that I love."

As if a volcano or a geyser had erupted inside of her, Aviva broke into heavy sobs, and her body completely gave out.

Erik held her upright, and let her cry against him for a moment, then kissed her, forcefully and deeply. She resisted him at first, or told herself that she did. But slowly, finally, she gave in. She kissed him back, and it was as if nothing had ever transpired between them, except for this longing, except for this love. Together, they sank to the floor.

Part 4:
Goodbye to the Dark

22

Aviva and Erik stayed in the abandoned home for several hours, making love in the stranger's bed, eating the stranger's food. Erik found a man's shirt that was too small for him, but he couldn't continue walking around in his military clothes. He and Aviva hid his German officer's uniform in a crawl space under the bed, the Nazi pin still attached to the shirt collar.

It was late in the afternoon now, and they walked cautiously down the streets of what had been the International Settlement. Armed Japanese soldiers stood at attention on every street corner. On every standing building soared a rising sun flag, and on every available wall hung posters that read *Premises under Military Control*. Almost every block had at least one pile of rubble, and they passed by an older couple digging through one pile of it, looking for their lost possessions.

One soldier appeared to be responsible for roaming the streets and yelling into a bullhorn a single message over and over: "All foreign citizens are now under Imperial occupation and subject to military rule. Business should be conducted as usual."

When Aviva and Erik reached the road that had always been the unofficial border between the International Settlement and the rest of the city, they saw that a long wooden and barbwire barrier had been erected. A Dutch woman wearing an armband was at the barrier trying to go out, but the armed guards refused to let her pass. She said that her husband and son were waiting for her at the docks, and that their boat would be leaving soon. Aviva watched as the woman opened up her purse and tried to offer the guards some money, but still they waived her away.

The Dutch woman dumped everything in her purse out on to the ground, and pleaded with them to let her pass. The guards pretended as if she were invisible and ignored her, even when she got down on her knees and begged. Even when she started pounding her open hand against the ground. The Dutch woman's money was flying everywhere, but Aviva could see that the woman didn't care. She cried that her family was waiting for her. They would leave her in Shanghai if they had to, they had to get out. She started picking the bills up off the ground and ripping them up in frustration, tossing the now worthless shreds of paper at the guards like confetti. But the wind carried most of it away before it reached them, and they just laughed, and laughed, and laughed at her.

~

By now, Mick Ryan had been sitting in a cold, dank cell in the basement of Bridge House for several hours, chained to a wall. When he arrived he'd been marched past a row of cells, each one holding a man who looked like he'd been beaten within an inch of his life. He recognized some of Wen Li's comrades from the Resistance meeting. They were the most bloodied.

Mick spent the first hour wondering why Tomoto would simply dump him here and then leave, until whispers started traveling between cells that the Japanese had annexed the International Settlement, and Mick understood what Tomoto had meant. Too busy today for someone as worthless as Mick, too many foreign assets to seize. The prisoners continued exchanging information in whispers, and when the whispers grew too loud, a guard picked a cell at random and beat the man inhabiting it, and no one spoke again after that. He wondered if his boss would try to find him and get him out of here, but even as he thought of it, he knew it wouldn't happen.

He wasn't worthless. He had something Tomoto wanted. Information, locations. Whispers.

~

In the basement of Mr. Chen's Restaurant and Café, Chen and Wen Li lay on a makeshift pallet on the floor. Chen had half-carried, half-dragged Wen Li from their hiding place behind Bridge House all the way back home as the sun was coming up. Entering through the sewer door, Chen had been too exhausted to climb the basement steps, and the two men fell into a deep sleep for several hours on the floor. Little Tao had spent the morning in the kitchen with the aunties, who had decided to close down the restaurant since Mr. Chen was nowhere to be found, and there were no customers anyway. Finally, Little Tao had come into the basement and found them there on the floor, and had woken them up with the sharp chirp of his pet cricket in their ears.

Now Tao was bringing them large jugs of water, stood and watched as his father and Wen Li quickly gulped it down, then went dutifully up for more.

"I think you've recuperated enough," Chen said to Wen Li. "Now, we have to get you out of Shanghai."

Wen Li protested immediately, but Chen was firm.

"Someone must've seen us," Chen said. "And if any of your men were captured—"

He cut off as Wen Li coughed into a white linen napkin that Tao had brought down from the dining room. Chen watched, alarmed at the red spot of blood that seeped through. Wen Li tried to catch his breath before speaking.

"They would never betray me," he said.

Suddenly they heard voices and heavy footsteps in the kitchen above them, and Chen stood up in alarm. He'd sent the kitchen maids home; Tao was sitting next to him; he wasn't sure where Aviva had gone, if perhaps she had abruptly decided to leave Shanghai, like many were doing. The footsteps were too heavy to be hers.

Wen Li struggled into a standing position, and the both drew their knives, resigned to whatever or whoever was coming for them.

The basement door opened, and it *was* Aviva, and behind her a man that Chen didn't recognize, tall and very blond, almost blindingly white. They were holding hands. Tao ran to Aviva and she scooped him up into a hug, and Chen and Wen Li finally relaxed, though both of them regarded Aviva's friend with suspicion.

Aviva wound a fresh strip of gauze around Wen Li's stomach as Chen held him upright.

Erik stood awkwardly watching them from across the

room while Little Tao paced in front of him like a guard on duty, trying to look menacing up at the tall, yellow-haired stranger.

"What happened last night?" she asked Wen Li.

"Some of us were killed," he weakly replied. "Some of us were captured."

Aviva pulled a bandage tightly across Wen Li's skin to hold the gauze in place. "I saw Mick being arrested," she said. "Do you trust him?"

Wen Li let his head droop against his chest. She'd never seen him look this defeated.

"Trust is for times of peace," he said. "Not times of war."

Chen had barely taken his eyes from Erik, watching the man's every move. He remembered Aviva's words to him that night in the dining room, and how she'd begged him not to tell Rabbi Mesner anything. *I left my family, too*, she'd said.

"What did you say your friend's name was?" Chen spoke to Aviva, was looking at Erik.

She hadn't prepared herself for this, and started stammering some nonsensical reply until Erik spoke up.

"Hank," said Erik, in what Aviva assumed was

his best accent lifted from American films. "Just call me Hank."

Aviva had finished bandaging Wen Li, and Chen helped him return to a reclining position to keep the bleeding from starting up again.

"Hank?" Wen Li said softly, with knowing scoff.

Chen wiped his hands with a rag, eyes still dead on Erik, and echoed Wen Li. "Hank?" he mused. "Are you sure it isn't 'Hanz?'"

Both Aviva and Erik blanched, but said nothing, and she pulled Little Tao into a cradling hug.

"I've always liked German poetry," Wen Li with sincerity, seemingly finished with mocking Erik. "There's one by Ernst Toller, about war." He seemed to be speaking from a dream, his eyes not landing anywhere. "How does it go? *Wir Wand'rer zum Tode?*"

He purposely mispronounced one of the words — *tode*, death — and Erik corrected him, resigned to admitting his Germanness.

Wen Li smiled vaguely. He wanted to carry on with the poem, but they all could only remember the first few lines.

"We death bound wanderers…," said Wen Li.

Chen joined in. "...To the earth condemned."

"We unlaureled victims...," added Aviva.

Erik finished it. "...Prepared for our end."

~

Kiyata stood at attention at the doorway of Mick's cell as Tomoto strode toward him. Kiyata saluted him, but Tomoto only gave him a contemptuous glance before entering the cell.

Mick shifted fearfully as Tomoto approached him. Kiyata brought over a chair from a corner of the room and placed it directly in front of the their prisoner, and Captain Tomoto sat down it with a heavy, tired sigh.

"Rough day?" piped Mick.

The captain chuckled, he can't help himself. He enjoyed the young journalist's never-ending Americaness.

"Not rough, just busy," Tomoto said. "I should apologize. We've been neglecting you."

"Oh, I really don't mind..." Mick trailed off as they all waited for the sound of a blood-curdling scream coming from another cell to stop, then continued, "...really."

Tomoto chuckled again. "The truth is, I like you." He slapped his knee in a jovial, grandfatherly way. "Even though you're an idiot. Even though you're American. I find myself not really wanting to torture you." He gestured at Kiyata behind him. "Which, as the young lieutenant here would tell you, is quite rare."

Tomoto removed a square of paper from his pocket, unfolded it, and held it up so that he and Mick could study it together like tutor and student: the unfinished article from his typewriter.

Tomoto rolled the article up into a neat paper tube, leaned in close to Mick, and tapped the young man gently but menacingly on the head, the face, the throat, with every few words that he spoke.

"And that." Tap. "Is why." Tap. "You're going to stop fucking around." Tap, tap. "And tell me: where is Wen Li?"

23

In the basement of Mr. Chen's, Aviva studied Wen Li's old bloodied bandages wadded up in her hands. She looked mournfully at him lying there, his strength drained, and said softy, "Look at what you've done to yourself."

Wen Li struggled to sit up, indignant, and batted Chen away when he reached out to help him.

"Wouldn't you do the same thing?" he asked. "For your people, for your family? For your home?" He lay back down. "Shanghai's my home. And I'll never abandon it."

Erik came over to Aviva, but she moved away from him and went to the garbage can to throw the old bandages away. She looked at her hands. Wen Li's blood was on them.

Erik followed her over, and whispered into her ear. "We have to go now, Aviva." He started up the stairs.

Aviva started to follow him. Chen up picked Tao and carried him over to the stairwell, blocking her path.

"Do you remember what I said, Aviva?" Chen asked her, looking deeply into her face as if expecting to find the answer there. "About someone finding the evidence of who you truly are?"

She nodded. She was afraid to speak, afraid too many emotions would well up in her voice and scare Little Tao.

"The 'someone' can be yourself," said Chen. Then he put Tao back down and turned away from her, and went to sit with Wen Li.

She studied Mr. Chen for a moment. He held a water jug up to Wen Li's mouth, patiently waiting as the young man—who was possibly dying—drank.

Little Tao was staring up at her, a child waiting for something to happen.

She leaned down and wiped a finger across his dirty cheek, and said, "I'll be right back."

Erik was pacing anxiously around the kitchen as Aviva came upstairs. As soon she closed the door behind her, he grabbed her waist and pulled her to him, talking in an excited rush, not noticing the look of reluctance on her face.

"Erik," she began slowly, but he was already talking over her.

"We've got to make it to the docks soon," he was saying, "before they—"

"Stop!" She was harsher, louder than she'd meant to be. "Stop," she said again, softer now. She laid three fingers gently on his mouth, not only to keep him from speaking, but so that she couldn't see the curl of the smile that always waiting for her there.

She started again. "I can't go—"

The loud roar of an engine filled her ears, as if a car had driven right into the dining room. Aviva and Erik rushed to the swinging doors, and through the large dining room windows they saw a plain military truck pulling up outside in front of the restaurant.

Erik backed away from the doors in a panic.

"It's the General!" he cried. "They've come for me. They've tracked me here."

He looked like he was about to fall over, and Aviva took him by the shoulders to steady him. He seemed not to see her, looking wildly around the kitchen. A trapped deer.

"They'll shoot me for desertion," he was saying now, not to Aviva, but to himself. "I'll be shot."

Aviva didn't know what to do, and found herself looking down at Erik as he sank to his knees in front of her.

"Please," he said, his handsome face filled with fear and desperation. "Hide me."

As Aviva led Erik to a closet in the kitchen, beneath them Chen, Wen Li, and Little Tao had heard the roar of the engine, too.

"It's Tomoto," said Chen. He looked at Wen Li. "You have to get out. Can you walk?"

"I can try," he said, and painfully pulled himself up.

Chen motioned for Tao to come and help him, and together they led Wen Li to the sewer door.

"Go with him until he's out of the International Settlement," Chen told Tao, "then come right back." It pained him to place such sudden responsibility on the boy. But Chen had to stay behind. If Tomoto had finally come to him, then that meant that it was time. He had his own mission to complete, his own promise to fulfill. His own questions that demanded answers.

Chen watched as Wen Li hobbled forward into the darkness, and just like that, his friend was gone.

Overhead, he heard a thunder of footsteps clamoring into his restaurant. Through the dining room. Into the kitchen. Now, coming down the basement stairs.

Just as Aviva was pulling the closet door closed, Lieutenant Kiyata and two of his officers burst into the kitchen.

Aviva left the door open the tiniest crack that she could, and she and Erik watched as the three Japanese men went straight for the basement door. As if they knew exactly where to look.

"No!" Aviva gasped softly, and Erik immediately shushed her. They could hear a scuffle downstairs, and a moment later saw a handcuffed Mr. Chen being dragged up into the kitchen by the officers.

These were no German generals. They were here for Mr. Chen, not for Erik. Aviva watched as Mr. Chen tried to straighten himself up, but one of the officers gave him a swift punch to the gut, he doubled over in pain. Aviva could hardly recognize Chen's face, all of his dignity stolen from him.

"We can't let them," she whispered, and put a

hand to the doorknob.

Erik swiftly wrapped himself around her, pinning her into a vice grip from behind. He put a hand over her mouth, and whispered harshly into her ear.

"Shut. Up."

Lieutenant Kiyata came upstairs from the basement.

"He isn't here," he said to his officers.

They picked Chen up off of the floor and led him out through the dining room. Kiyata hung back for a few moments, surveying the kitchen.

Inside the closet, Erik tightened his grip on Aviva, until she whimpered softly in pain. Through the crack in the door, they both watched as Kiyata glanced around once more. Then he was gone.

A few moments later they heard the truck roar to life and speed away. Erik finally relaxed his grip on her, and like a wild animal suddenly freed from a trap, she sprang away from him.

24

Aviva rushed to the basement stairs.

Erik called after her. "We'll miss the boat!" he said. "And then I'll be trapped here."

She ignored him. Her shoulders throbbed where his arms had gripped her. The skin around her mouth where his hand had been now felt raw. How many times had she let him touch her? She would never touch him again.

The basement was empty. No Tao, no Wen Li. She came back up into the kitchen and found Erik once more pacing at the stairs. She brushed past him.

"They're gone," she said, more to herself than to him. To him, she had nothing left to say. She heard the rasp of his voice in her ear, louder than the sound of Mr. Chen's groans as he was being beaten right in front of her. *Shut up*.

"Of course they're gone," said Erik, exasperated. "Aviva, are you blind? Everyone is trying to leave Shanghai right now, and so should we."

His voice was only background noise to her thoughts. Wen Li was injured, he wasn't strong enough to take care of Tao. Where could they be? She went to the alley door as Erik went on.

"The same thing that's happening at home," Erik was saying, "in Germany, in France, is on it's way here. It's *already* here!"

Aviva stopped. She turned back around to face Erik, the man who, just a few hours before, she had convinced herself she could love.

That was over.

But Erik knew things. He knew about the Japanese seizing the Settlement, he knew which ships were leaving the harbor for America, which sailors could be bribed, which borders could be crosses. She thought he'd already told her everything. But now she suddenly knew that he hadn't.

"What do you mean?" she asked solemnly, dreading the answer. *"What's* already here?"

Erik explained to her what every German and Japanese officer knew. The Emperor and the Fuhrer had come to a sort of agreement. All citizens of enemy countries in Shanghai would be rounded up and placed into camps. Work camps, he supposed. When? Soon. Germany wanted the fate of the Jews of Shanghai to be turned over to German consulate, but the Japanese had been resisting the proposal, or rather, the veiled demand.

But there was a compromise afoot. Japan had agreed to move the entire Jewish population of the city into a single ghetto, where they could be closely monitored.

When? He didn't know. Soon.

"That's why we need to go to the harbor, *now*," said Erik. "I don't want anything bad to happen to *you*. I want to keep you safe."

Aviva could barely hear him. She was thinking of Rabbi Mesner and all of the refugees. She had to tell him, to warn him. But not with Erik by her side.

She realized that he was looking expectantly at her, as if he'd posed some question and was waiting on an answer. She knew that he needed to believe that this was really all about her, that all of his escapes, all of the grand schemes, were out of his love for her. Not his shiftlessness, not his indolence.

The only that she could get to the synagogue was if she could get away from Erik. And the only way that she could remove herself from his grip was to play along. Lie down in the grass, and let the hunter approach, and open the trap for you.

"We'd better get going," said Aviva, her voice soft and sweet.

Erik sprang into action. "I've just got to find the right man," he said, "the right sailor to let us aboard." The childlike glitter in his eyes had returned. Time for an adventure.

But when Aviva told Erik that he should go ahead to the harbor, and that she would meet him there, his eyes instantly narrowed. He asked why.

"For my valise," was her reply. It was at the synagogue, and she needed to go collect it, and surely he could understand why he couldn't come with her. Yes, it really *was* important. Didn't he remember the diary she'd kept? It was locked away in her little red trunk, and she couldn't leave without it.

She would meet him later, at the harbor.

Of course, darling.

She would be there.

~

In the basement of Bridge House, Kiyata led Mr. Chen down the hallway to what would be his cell. Chen looked at every man as he passed. He saw some of Wen Li's comrades, he saw Mick. Mick Ryan was the only one who did not look severely bloodied and bruised, though somehow the air around him was more defeated. He looked away as Chen walked past.

Chen momentarily stopped walking, realizing what Mick's clean face really meant, that he was the one who'd revealed Wen Li's whereabouts. *Do you trust him?* Aviva had asked.

One of Kiyata's soldiers jabbed Chen in the back with his bayonet, urging him forward, but Kiyata stopped him.

"Go on, Mr. Chen," he said gently to the restaurant owner, who had always been gracious, who had always been kind. "Go on."

Tomoto stood in his office, the scorched walls still filling the room with the smell of soot. He'd taken his old *kendo* sword down from its decorative ledge — *what good was a sword behind glass?* he wanted to know — and was going through his old routines when Kiyata appeared at his door.

"Mr. Chen is ready, sir," said Kiyata.

Tomoto didn't respond, only continued raising the sword and lowering it slowly in precise patterns. Kiyata realized the captain was barefoot.

"Do you know why a fighter receives this sword?" he asked Kiyata, holding it up so that the younger man could inspect its quality. "To award a man for —"

"Honor, sir," Kiyata said, cutting him off.

Tomoto studied him for a moment, then looked away.

"This Chen," drawled Tomoto. "He's...?" Tomoto trails off, then finally looked back at Kiyata, waiting for him to fill in the blank.

"The husband of Su Chen," said the lieutenant. "Yes. It's him."

Tomoto crossed the room and looked out of the window that had yet to be repaired after Wen Li's little raid. A few broken shards were still attached to the window frame, and Tomoto gently poked them out with the tip of his sword.

"Are you going to question Chen now?" Kiyata asked. "About Wen Li?" He remained standing in the doorframe, no desire to be invited in.

Tomoto turned back around to face him. "No," he said, looking hard at Kiyata. "You do it."

Kiyata stared back at him in shock. He didn't do that, not what Tomoto did. He pulled triggers when triggers needed pulling, he lit cannons when cannons needed lighting. He wasn't Tomoto. Not yet. If he ever began to go down that road, he vowed to himself that he would send his pacifist parents one long, final letter, then throw himself into a fire, or into the sea. Kiyata saluted his captain, and turned to go.

"And Kiyata?" Tomoto called out.

The lieutenant stopped just outside of the door, but didn't turn around.

Tomoto spoke to his back. "Be thorough."

A young Kempeitai officer held Chen up by the throat, and punched him in his already bloodied face. His neck hung loosely and lolled back and forth, but he was still conscious. The soldier let him go, and he dropped to the floor.

Kiyata stood at the door.

"Where is Wen Li?" he asked, speaking in rote fashion. He had, in fact, been asking the same question now, in the same emotionless manner, for what felt like hours, but was really only several minutes. He hadn't laid a finger on Mr. Chen. Kiyata had made it clear that he only needed one thing from him, that hurting him was not his goal. Chen spat out a mouthful of blood.

"Where's Tomoto?" he cried out, sounding maniacal even to his own ears. "I came to see Tomoto!"

Chen saw Kiyata and the soldier exchange a glance.

"Doesn't Tomoto want to do this to me himself?" Chen asked.

The soldier again looked at Kiyata, but the lieutenant locked eyes with Chen.

"No," said Kiyata. "He doesn't."

The lieutenant breathed a heavy sigh. Then nodded curtly at the soldier, his face filled with regret.

The soldier went to Mr. Chen, and began again.

25

It was evening now, and Aviva pushed her way through the crowded streets, trying to hold her ground as people swarmed past her. She was moving against the flow, away from the harbor, while everyone else was going toward it.

When she arrived to the synagogue, she stopped to take in the large stone building, the way she always did. She looked around for the friendly chalkboard welcome sign, but it was gone.

She found Rabbi Mesner's office door open, but no one inside. Somehow the room seemed larger, and she realized it was because the many stacks of luggage were no longer there. She remembered when she'd first caught sight of her valise in here. The panic that had struck her then, so fearful of what he might learn of her if he looked inside.

But for the past three days, she hadn't thought of it, not once. So much had happened, truer dangers kept becoming known. Still, the lie to Erik had rolled so cleanly off her tongue, as if the diary and the little red trunk had only been waiting for her to remember them.

"What are you doing here?" a voice said from behind her.

She quickly turned around, startled. But it was only Rabbi Mesner, and she smiled.

He didn't smile back. "Are you looking for something?" he asked in a strange voice.

"Nothing," she stammered. "I mean, no." Why was he looking at her like that? She had arrived with the vigor of an emissary, but the feeling was quickly waning. "I have to tell you something. Something's going to happen—"

The rabbi cut her off as he went to his desk, keeping a wide birth between them and avoiding her eyes.

"No money coming in from America," he said with a dismissive wave of his hand. "I know, I know."

He sat down, and Aviva realized he was ringing his hands. He looked half-angry, half-pleading.

"But, my child. My Aviva," he said, "what I need to know is this: what are you truly looking for? Why are you really here?"

Aviva didn't understand what the rabbi was talking about. She stared at him with genuine confusion, even while a more knowing dread crept up in her. The way he was looking at her now, it was familiar. It was an exact match to how, for the last three months, she'd felt about herself.

She opened her mouth to answer him, not even knowing yet what would come out. But Mrs. Borgrov rushed in. She ignored Aviva, and spoke hurriedly to the rabbi.

"Come quick!" she said. "There isn't enough rice today, not by half. They're fighting for it."

Rabbi Mesner jumped up and rushed out with

Borgrov, passing by Aviva without a look or a word.

For a moment, Aviva remained there, alone. Who did she have in this whole world? She'd thought Samuel, she'd thought Erik, she'd thought, in a different way, Rabbi Mesner.

But then she remembered: she hadn't come here to talk about herself. She wasn't here to relive her past or wallow in the present. She had something important to say, and the rabbi would hear it from her, whether he suddenly hated her or not.

Aviva wound her way through the chaotic cafeteria. She spotted Mrs. Borgrov walking hurriedly by carrying a large but deflated sack of rice, more than half empty.

"What's going on?" she asked the older woman.

Borgrov didn't slow down, and Aviva had to trot to keep up.

"What's going on?" the Polish woman exclaimed. "Well, half of the people we'd gotten homes for found themselves living in a pile of rubble today. So they're all back now. *That's* what's going on."

"Where is Rabbi Mesner?" she asked.

Borgrov responded with a gasp of exasperation.

"Can you not see how busy—"

Aviva stopped trotting, and put a firm hand on Borgrov's arm, forcing her to stop, too.

"Please," Aviva said. This was no time for petty rivalries. "It's urgent."

Borgrov took in the earnestness on Aviva's pleading face.

"Alright, alright," said the woman in a softer but still exasperated tone. "Calm down already."

As Borgrov led her through the various halls searching for Rabbi Mesner, she tried to take in every refugee's face as she passed them, and the anguish she felt grew with every step.

They found the rabbi in a corner doling out instruction to volunteers. As Aviva approached he glanced at her and said, "You again?"

"I must speak with you," she said firmly, undaunted, holding his gaze.

"I'm afraid I can't," he returned immediately. "Too many people need my help today, and you are not on of those people." He went back to his work, then said more quietly, "Perhaps you never were."

She thought she had steeled herself against this, but she hadn't.

For the second or third time that day, angry tears welled up in her as she tried to get a man to stop talking, to just shut his mouth, and listen to her.

She kept her voice steady, and told him that everyone around them would be in greater danger tomorrow than they were today.

Now Borgrov and the young volunteers gasped at Aviva's words, and the rabbi had no choice but to consider her. He asked her what she meant.

"Not here," she said, casting a subtle nod at the volunteers nearest her, who were basically still teenagers and who had been hanging on their every word. "We should speak privately." She gestured to Borgrov. "The three of us."

The rabbi nodded slowly, and said that yes, the three of them did in fact have something important to discuss. Aviva relaxed a little; Rabbi Mesner seemed to be coming around.

As the trio walked together toward his office, he studied the back of Aviva's pretty head, and wondered what lies would spring from it now.

~

Kiyata watched with alarm as blood poured from Chen's face. His nose, his eyes, his mouth. The young soldier leaned back, as if to admire his work, stepping right into a small pool of the prisoner's blood. Kiyata checked the soldier's face. Was he enjoying this? Had Tomoto told *him* to be thorough, in case Kiyata wasn't?

On the floor, Chen groaned.

Kiyata ordered the soldier to go and find something to clean up the mess. The soldier saluted him, leaving a smear of blood on his forehead. As soon as he was gone, Kiyata kneeled in front of Mr. Chen. He took his own kerchief from his pocket, and instead of giving it to the bloodied man to wipe his own face, he wiped it for him.

"Please," Kiyata whispered. He didn't want to risk being overheard by the other prisoners, or by a passing soldier. "We can end this now. Just give the captain something," he said. "Anything."

Chen's eyes were starting to swell shut, but he could see Su kneeling next to Kiyata, smiling down at him encouragingly.

"Tomoto has already taken everything from me," Chen groaned. "I have nothing left to give him."

Kiyata shook the older man in frustration.

"You know what I mean," Kiyata growled. "Wen Li! That's who Tomoto wants."

Chen looked around for Su, but she had already disappeared. He looked back to Kiyata.

"All he wants is Wen Li?" Chen asked.

"Yes," he said. "Where is he?

Chen did not answer, but pulled himself to his feet. "Release me."

Kiyata stood, too. "You know I can't do that," he said. "Not until you tell—"

"Tell Tomoto," said Chen, "that I'll get a message to Wen Li to meet me somewhere in the city. He'll come, if it's from me."

Kiyata balked, but Chen pressed on. "You and Tomoto can come there, and arrest him. But only the two of you. No one else."

Kiyata studied him. The mad laughter was gone now. The strange smiles he'd been casting at empty spaces had disappeared.

"He'll never agree to this," said Kiyata.

"Well, then," said Chen, brazen now, "I'll need you to convince him."

~

Rabbi Mesner and Mrs. Borgrov sat in grief-stricken shock. The rabbi knew what it meant in Germany, when their government had started to shuffle all the Jews into a single neighborhood, then into a single block, then into a single building. Mrs. Borgrov knew what it meant in Poland, when entire Jewish families disappeared all at once into what were *called* work camps, but were really a holding place for the living dead.

But this was China. This was Shanghai. What did it mean *here*?

"And you're sure?" said Mrs. Borgrov.

"Yes," Aviva said. "I'm sure."

Rabbi Mesner abruptly got up from his desk and began to pace the room, muttering to himself. Then just as suddenly, he stopped, and turned on Aviva.

"When?" he asked sharply.

"I don't, I don't know," she stammered back. "Soon."

Borgrov breathed a heavy sigh. "Thank goodness you've warned us—"

But the rabbi cut her off. "And how did you find out about this plan," he said, eyeing her with blatant suspicion, "between Germans and Japanese?"

Aviva stared at him, but didn't answer.

Couldn't answer.

"That doesn't matter," Mrs. Borgrov said, to Aviva's surprise. The woman looked directly at her and said again, "It doesn't matter how."

But the rabbi would not be deterred. He wanted answers, he needed them. He didn't understand it himself, why he was so angry with this girl in front of him. But he was.

"Did you learn of it from your German boyfriend?" he asked. He voice had fallen to practically a whisper, as if the words that were coming were physically painful to say. "Did your Nazi lover tell you this?"

As soon as the question passed his lips, he knew with complete clarity that he wanted her to say no. He wanted her to admit to nothing, to deny everything. That diary, it belonged to someone else. That photo, it wasn't of her. If she said this, he would believe her. He would take her at her word. They would put their heads together, the three of them, and figure out how to navigate this treacherous new world that they thought they had all escaped, but was now springing up around them again. *Say no*, he thought, watching her. *Say no*.

Aviva had imagined this moment from the very first day she arrived. She had turned it over, and over, in her head. And now, here it was.

"Yes," she said, willing herself to look directly at Rabbi Mesner as she spoke. "I learned it from him."

Aviva had never seen a man look so deflated. She'd seen her husband worried over how he was going to save their lives; she'd seen Wen Li practically dying in front of her on this very day. The rabbi shuffled back to his desk and sat down, as if everything in him had depended on her answer to his question, and her answer had failed him.

Mrs. Borgrov took over. "And your husband, his name was Samuel? And your daughter, Ora?" She posed these questions with the simplicity of a census taker. Not warm, but not unkind. "Where are they now?"

Whatever composure Aviva had up to this point threatened to flee from her.

She drew a breath and said she didn't know.

The rabbi opened a drawer in his desk and pulled out her journal. On top of it was the photo of her and Samuel and Ora.

She wanted to snatch it up, but she didn't dare. She didn't know where to look, what to do, or say. Mrs. Borgrov seemed to be reading her mind.

"The truth, Aviva," she said gently. "Just say the truth."

The rabbi scoffed with contempt. He didn't think she was capable of truth.

His resentment sickened him.

He should have gotten remarried. He should've had a daughter. He would have taught her the difference between right and wrong, truth and lie. One was good, one was bad. Do the good thing, don't do the bad thing. How hard was that?

"The truth," Aviva began, "is that I loved them." She looked from the rabbi, to Borgrov, then back to the rabbi. "And if I knew where they were, I would go there right now, and I would give my life for theirs." She stood. "But I don't," she said. "And I can't."

She said goodbye to Mrs. Borgrov, who said it back, and goodbye to Rabbi Mesner, who didn't.

She reached the door just as a group of young volunteers were passing by in the hallway, giggling in their bright blue shirts. They stuck their hands through the doorframe, waving at the three adults inside. *Hello!* Hello.

Aviva looked back at Rabbi Mesner and Mrs. Borgrov. "I hope you can protect them," Aviva said. "From what may be coming."

In the hallway she wanted to break into a run. But she didn't. Where had running ever gotten her? Only back to where she'd begun.

Just as Aviva was exiting the synagogue for the final time, she heard Mrs. Borgrov behind her, calling her name.

The stout Polish woman broke into a jog to catch up to her, as if she thought Aviva might disappear onto the street.

Now the woman was leaning against the ornately carved synagogue doors and catching her breath.

"When you came into the shop that day," Borgrov said. "Do you remember?"

Aviva nodded, of course she remembered.

Mrs. Borgrov said that on that morning, she'd received a letter from Poland, from her brother. Before this, she hadn't heard from him in over a year. He'd been in a prison camp, and had somehow escaped, and one of the first things he'd done was write to his older sister all the way in Shanghai.

Aviva said that that was wonderful, and Borgrov told her not to interrupt.

In the letter, Borgrov said, her brother wrote that he'd seen people being burned alive in the camp.

"And when I read that," Borgrov continued, "I felt guilty." She put a hand on the younger woman's shoulder. "Because my first thought was not, 'how horrible that people were burned alive.' My first thought was, 'thank god that *I* am still alive, and not *there*, burning with them.'"

Mrs. Borgrov pulled something from the pocket of her dress and handed it to Aviva. It was her journal. Borgrov started back inside.

"But do you still feel it?" Aviva asked her. "That guilt?"

Mrs. Borgrov shrugged one shoulder carelessly, almost girlish.

"It stays with us, yes. The guilt, the shame, the relief," Borgrov said. "We have to live with it, Aviva. But, we get to live."

Mrs. Borgrov said goodbye, and went inside, and closed the heavy synagogue doors behind her.

Aviva looked at the journal in her hand, fanned through the pages, and found the photo.

She started to pluck it out, when suddenly Erik was in front of her, grabbing the journal out of her hand.

"Is this it?" he said, looking it over. "Are you ready? Can we go now?"

She was too startled to answer. Where had he come from, had he been watching her this whole time? She snatched the book back from him.

"I told you not to follow me," she said, panicked. Would she ever be rid of him? Could she ever go for a walk and not find him there, waiting for her in the shadows?

He took her hand into his. "And I told you that I won't let you slip away."

They started down the street, him leading her toward the harbor, and she kept her eyes staring straight ahead, seeing nothing. "Not ever," he said. "Not ever again."

26

Chen stood at one end of a long, empty alley at the edge of the International Settlement, looking up into the night sky, as if savoring his last moments on earth.

He listened as a car pulled up at the other end of the alley. He heard the car door open, the door slam shut, footsteps. But he didn't turn around.

"So, this is Mr. Chen," said Captain Tomoto. "Of Mr. Chen's Restaurant."

Now, Chen turned around.

"And café," Chen added.

Tomoto was several yards away from him. Behind him, Kiyata remained in the car, watching them.

Chen took a step toward Tomoto.

"One year ago," he began, "you left Shanghai and went back to Japan." He stepped forward again. "But you took something with you that belonged to me. My wife."

Tomoto took a few steps to Chen, grinning at him.

"Ah," said Tomoto, "but can a woman ever truly belong to a man?"

Chen inched forward as he spoke.

"Perhaps not. But I belonged to her," he said. "And our son, Little Tao. He belonged to her." Chen was close enough now to lock eyes with Tomoto, and he studied the man before him. "You never had sons, did you?"

Tomoto's grin quickly turned to grimace.

"I came here to arrest Wen Li," he said, "not listen to sad stories about dead women."

Chen stopped a foot away from Tomoto.

"I came here to ask you one question," Chen said. "My wife. Su. Did she—"

Chen broke off. It felt like he was choking on something. Tomoto put one hand to his holster as Chen went on.

"Did she go with you, or did you force her?" he said in a rush. "Did she love you? Did you love her?"

Tomoto tried to imagine what Chen's life must be like. He had a child, a son. He had one tiny kingdom where he both lived and worked, and where he was king.

"Mr. Chen, I'm afraid you've made a horrible mistake," said Tomoto. "You see, that was three questions."

Tomoto whipped the pistol from his holster. But he wasn't fast enough.

Chen was already on him. They wrestled for the gun, and Chen came out on top. He straddled Tomoto, holding his face against the concrete with one hand and pointing the captain's own gun at his head with the other.

Seeing his boss apparently defeated, Kiyata started up the car, and drove off.

The sound of the engine caused Chen to look up, and Tomoto tried to grab the gun away. But Chen kept his grip on it, and so did Tomoto.

Tomoto yanked a short blade from his holster, and stabbed Chen twice in his side. He cried out in pain, but finally managed to yank the gun from Tomoto's grip. He placed the barrel of the captain's gun right on top of his temple.

For a moment, the two stared eye-to-eye, until finally Tomoto dropped his knife in surrender.

"What do you want from me?" he growled. "She's dead."

Chen wondered if there was any humanity left in the man beneath him. He wondered if just by holding this man's gun to this man's head, his own humanity was being drained from him.

"The truth," said Chen. "All I want is the truth."

Tomoto looked up at Chen and tried not let the fear show in his face. He knew when he was in the presence of a killer, and he knew that Chen wasn't one. But still, Tomoto was on the ground, and Chen had the gun.

"The truth is exactly what you think," Tomoto said. "I took her from you."

Chen said nothing, so Tomoto went on.

"The day I left for Tokyo, I saw her walking in the street. I dragged her onto the ship by her hair." He had never done this before, discussed a woman in this way with another man. He was enjoying it. "Come to think of it, I remember her crying out your name," said Tomoto. "I think she was calling for you to come and save her."

A primal scream erupted from deep inside of Chen. He whipped the butt of the pistol across Tomoto's face. Once, then twice, then a third time, until he couldn't find the strength to raise his arm again.

Blood streamed across Tomoto's face. He grinned up at Chen, the blood staining his teeth.

After Chen had caught his breath, he asked Tomoto if he had killed her.

"She poisoned herself," Tomoto said. He tried to spit out a mouthful of blood, but Chen wouldn't allow him to raise his head, and so it dribbled across his cheek. "She mixed it herself and drank it, and then she got into bed with me. She wanted me to watch her die." Tomoto laughed, and it turned into a deep, racking cough. "That's how much she hated me."

Chen pulled himself off of Tomoto and stood, still aiming the gun at him.

"Go," Chen said.

But Tomoto didn't move an inch. He eyed Chen suspiciously from his spot on the ground.

"Go," he said again. "I told you, I just wanted the truth."

Tomoto got up, but still, he didn't walk away. Chen told him not to worry, that he wouldn't shoot him in the back.

"No?" said Tomoto. "I would."

Tomoto finally turned from Chen, and walked slowly down the alley. He practically sauntered, daring Chen to raise the gun. To pull the trigger. To put him out of his misery.

27

By the time, Aviva and Erik arrived at the harbor, she knew what she had to do. No more games, no more traps. In a way, they both were the deer.

Just ahead of them stood a long line of people boarding a passenger ship, everyone trying desperately to get to the front of the queue.

"That's ours," whispered Erik.

But several armed German and Japanese soldiers were managing the crowd, checking faces and asking for passports. They all seemed to be taking orders from one German general, a short, portly man standing atop a platform overlooking the crowd.

When Erik spotted the general, his eyes widened in fear and his face went white. Aviva remembered how he'd panicked in the kitchen. *They'll shoot me for desertion*, he'd said. *I'll be shot.*

Erik pulled Aviva with him and they inched forward through the crowd toward the ship. He kept his head turned away from the general, so that even though Erik could not see him, he also could not be seen.

But Aviva kept her eyes on the portly man atop the platform. She was waiting for him to throw a glance in their direction. All she needed was for the general to look over at them.

And then he did.

Aviva broke away from Erik, and ran straight for the general. Erik instinctually followed her, and by the time he realized the direction in which she was headed, it was too late. The general had spotted the tall blond body darting toward him in the crowd, and soon he was raising a bullhorn to his lips, and Erik's name filled the air.

"Von Strommer! Erik von Strommer!"

A dozen German soldiers surrounded him all at once. Aviva had melted into the crowd, but she was still close enough to see the terror on Erik's face. She had to look away.

The thronging mass of people propelled her toward the ships. But she wasn't leaving Shanghai. She managed to push her way out of the crowd, and began walking in the opposite direction of the harbor, toward home. She looked back only once, at the boats pushing off from the docks, new boats coming in. Desperate people climbing past each other to board one. Any one.

28

Tomoto burst through the front door of Bridge House and stalked down the hallway toward his office, ignoring the officers staring at his bruised face, his bloody clothes.

At the door of his office, two soldiers stood at attention. He grabbed one of them by the collar.

"Kiyata," he glowered, "where is he?"

The soldiers were alarmed by their captain's beat-up appearance, and confused by his question. They looked helplessly at each other, and then back to Tomoto.

"Lieutenant Kiyata is with you, sir," said the soldier, sure that it was the correct answer, and for which he was rewarded with Tomoto slamming his head into the wall behind him.

Tomoto yanked the pistol from the holster of the other soldier, who immediately fell into a ball on he floor, sure that his captain was going to shoot him. But Tomoto was already striding back down the hall.

He stopped abruptly, and went back to his office, the soldiers cowering as he passed. He took his sword down from the wall, unsheathed it, and stalked back out.

~

Chen staggered down the street, stopping every now and then to look down at his stomach. Tomoto's knife had gone deeper into him than he'd realized; his shirt was soaked through with blood.

For several more blocks he lurched forward unsteadily. He stopped again and leaned over to catch his breath. He cried out in pain. He looked up and saw his restaurant, just a few more blocks ahead.

He tried to take another step toward home, but finally he collapsed, clutching his wound. He felt exposed there, lying in the middle of the empty street. He crawled the few paces into the nearest alleyway, not seeing the trail of blood he was leaving behind him.

He curled himself against a wall, and told himself that he would just close his eyes. Just for a few moments, he would rest.

~

Aviva hurried down the street toward Mr. Chen's, unwittingly passing by Mr. Chen hidden in an alley, lying in a growing pool of his own blood.

Now she was in the dining room. Now she was in the kitchen. Everything was dark, and she called out names like a madwoman. Mr. Chen, Wen Li, Little Tao, were you there? No one answered her.

Finally, she sat down at the kitchen table, and put her head against the wood, exhausted.

Then, she heard a small, trilling chirp. She remained still, and strained her ears. There it was again. She followed the sound to one of the closets, opened the door, and found Tao sitting on the floor. He bounded into her arms and immediately started sobbing. How long had he been here alone? He shook his head, he didn't know.

"It's alright," she said soothingly. "I'm here. I won't leave you again."

Tomoto kicked open the door of the restaurant and strode into the dining room, a pistol in one hand, his sword in the other.

"Mr. Chen!" he bellowed into the dark, empty room. "Little Tao!"

He went to a wooden table in the center of the room, raised his sword, and brought it down, splitting the table into two.

"You have a customer!" he roared.

In the kitchen, Aviva quickly pulled Tao back into the closet where she'd found him, and shut the door. Inside it was pitch black. She couldn't see him, so she kneeled down and took his face into her hands. She made him promise not to leave this closet, no matter what he heard, no matter what happened.

"Promise me," she whispered, and felt Tao's tiny head nod in her hands.

Tomoto entered the kitchen.

His eyes immediately fell on the row of closet doors, and he went to the first one. Tomoto raised his sword, and thrust it through the door, retracted it, then looked peered through the hole he'd made: inside were shelves stacked dozens of cans and jars.

He moved to the next closet. Again he raised his sword and made a hole in the closet door: inside this one, a tangle of mops and brooms. As he peered through the hole, he heard a loud chirping noise emanating from the next closet over.

Inside the closet, Aviva hastily pushed Tao as far toward the back as possible, still cupping the cricket in his hands.

Tomoto went swiftly to the third closet, and raised his sword. Just as he was about to thrust it inside, the door opened, and Aviva came out. Tomoto immediately grabbed her by the throat.

"Where's Chen?" he demanded, and Aviva said she didn't know. His son, Tao? Again, she didn't know. Wen Li? Wen Li who?

Tomoto released her, and Aviva fell to the floor, gasping for breath.

He eyes roamed the kitchen. There were plenty of tools he could use on her: flames, boiling water, knives. None of them very subtle, but effective.

He glanced around the kitchen again, until his eyes landed on a lassoed rope, draped across a chair.

~

Chen lay on his back in the alley, his blood seeping into the ground.

Su was lying next to him, curled up close like they were in bed together, their faces almost touching. She pressed a hand gently to his wound, and he covered her hand with his own.

Now her lips were moving, no sound coming out that he could hear. She seemed worried about something, and her lips were silently repeating the same words, over and over.

Chen felt desperate to know what Su was saying.

"What wrong?" he asked her. "Tell me, please!"

Finally her voice rang clear.

"Save them," said Su. "Go and save them."

~

Tomoto sat calmly pointing his gun at Aviva, who was standing on top of a chair with the lasso tied into a noose around her neck, attached tautly to a beam overhead.

"Tell me where the boy is," Tomoto said.

Aviva stared down at him in silence, then said, "Tao is innocent."

Without a word in reply, Tomoto aimed his gun at one of the chair's front legs, and fired.

A fat wooden leg piece exploded away on impact. The chair immediately started to wobble, and Aviva let out a short cry, but quickly silenced herself. She shifted atop the chair, regaining her balance.

From inside the closet, Tao flinched at the sound of the gun shot, and the cricket jumped out of his hands.

"Nobody is innocent in war," said Tomoto.

~

Slowly, Chen dragged himself to his feet, and staggered out of the alleyway back onto the street. As he made his way to the restaurant, a gunshot rang out from inside, then another. With what felt like his last remaining ounce of strength, he broke out into a jog, and then he was running.

~

Her chair had only two legs remaining now, a front and a back leg on opposite sides.

Aviva stood there, her eyes closed serenely, as if she was already resigned to her fate. So this was how it would be. After everything she'd done, had done to others, had allowed others to do to her. Was this how she would say goodbye to the dark?

Tomoto regarded her thoughtfully. She was stronger than he had expected.

"If I asked you the same question again," he mused, "would you give me the same answer?"

Aviva opened her eyes and looked down on Tomoto.

"I would tell you the truth," she said.

He raised his pistol, and aimed it at the remaining front leg.

"Where are they?" he asked her.

"I don't know," she said, and the words are barely out of her mouth before Tomoto blasted away the third leg, and the chair collapsed from under her.

Her throat closed. Her thin legs danced violently in the air. Her fingers flew to the rope at her neck, trying to pull it away from her skin.

But the rope had become her skin.

Inside the closet, Tao sat with his hands over his eyes and his pet cricket on his knee.

The cricket chirped, and suddenly heavy footsteps were heading straight toward him.

Tomoto had one hand on the closet door when Chen burst into the kitchen. He rushed to Aviva and grabbed her legs, struggling to hold her up.

Tomoto lunged at him, pistol in hand, and together they toppled to the floor. Chen banged Tomoto's hand against the ground until his fingers weakened and began to bleed, and the pistol went scattering across the kitchen floor.

Aviva's face was now red, now purple. Now growing in size as her eyes and cheeks bulged outward.

Chen kicked Tomoto off of him and tried to get back to her, but Tomoto grabbed him from behind, pulling him away from Aviva.

As her body started to still, Tomoto hooked his arm around Chen's neck, and squeezed.

Chen tried to reach behind him, but he could only claw at Tomoto's face as he felt his own body quickly weakening. His feet thrashed around as he tried to free himself from Tomoto's grip, and he kicked something that crashed to the floor with a loud clang.

A sword.

Tomoto let go of Chen, and lunged for it.

But Chen got to the sword first, turned to Tomoto, and stuck it deep into the Japanese captain's chest.

He quickly yanked the sword from Tomoto's body and rushed to Aviva. Her face was already blank, and her feet had started to shake.

Chen raised the sword, still warm with Tomoto's blood, and sliced the rope.

Aviva fell limply into his arms.

As a man, Little Tao would remember the sound of his father's muffled sobs through the closet door. He would recall the exact number of minutes it had taken him to open the closet door, breaking his promise to Aviva only to find her motionless body and his father trying desperately to shake her awake. He would remember the number of deals he made with himself regarding when he would be allowed to speak. By the time Little Tao died at the age of ninety-two, there had been over three thousand four hundred and seventy-eight deals. All of which he'd lost.

ABOUT THE AUTHOR

Chidelia R. Edochie is an American writer living in Shanghai, China.

NOTES ON FACT & FICTION

The historical context of this novel is quite real: the exodus of European Jews to perceived "safe havens" like Shanghai and other cities in the Far East; the occupation of Shanghai by the Empire of Japan as part of a very long war with China; the "immunity" of the International Settlement and the huge departure from this status quo that erupted upon the bombing of Pearl Harbor and declarations of war between Japan, America, and Great Britain.

But all else a creation of my own, including Aviva and Erik, Mr. Chen and his restaurant, noble Wen Li, and Little Tao. All historical events have been heavily fictionalized, timelines have been greatly shifted, and the web of story has been spun.

That is to say, that this is a work of fiction. Names, characters, businesses, places, events and incidents are either the products of the author's imagination or used in a fictitious manner. Any resemblance to actual persons, living or dead, or actual events is purely coincidental.

PUBLIC DOMAIN USAGE

I have quoted Ernst Toller's poem, "Marching Song," which was first published in *Die Aktion, Wochenschrift für Politik, Literatur und Kunst* by the German editor Franz Pfemfert on May 6, 1918, and is now in the public domain.

Made in the USA
San Bernardino, CA
16 October 2016